"Women don't walk aw

No, she'd bet not. Most likely he gave them one heavy-lidded stare or a flash of that cocky grin and their panties melted off as they begged him for anything he was willing to give.

"I'm not walking away from you," she defended. "I'm walking away from this conversation."

"That's not fair." He took a half step closer. "I guarantee you know more about me than I know about you."

"That's not my fault you parade your life in front of the camera. You know all you need to in order for me to do my job."

He held her arm and ran his thumb along the inside of her elbow.

"You don't look like a nanny," he murmured, studying her face.

Her entire body heated. With each stroke of his thumb she felt the zings all over.

"What do I look like?" she asked. Why did that come out as a whisper?

"Like trouble."

* * *

A Texan for Christmas is part of Harlequin Desire's #1 bestselling series, Billionaires and Babies: Powerful men...wrapped around their babies' little fingers.

Dear Reader,

If you've been keeping up with my Rancher's Heirs series, you have already met Colt, Nolan and Hayes. Who's next? Oh, that's right. The mysterious Hollywood heartthrob, Beau Elliott.

I hope you'll forgive that I skipped ahead in this fictitious world and picked up where Hayes's book left off, but I made the season Christmas. What's more magical than Christmas? Believe me, these characters needed some magic in their lives!

Scarlett has suffered so much heartache, and being thrust into this nanny position is just another layer of pain. But working with Beau Elliott does help take out the sting. Who wouldn't want to be under the same roof with an A-list actor for three weeks?

Beau can't believe this is his nanny. Maybe he should've specified a warty, gray-haired grandmother, because the second the sultry Scarlett shows up on his doorstep, he knows he's in trouble. Poor Beau.

Once these two break past the barriers of heartache and pain, they quickly realize they have more in common than they ever thought possible. And with the magic of Christmas and a beautiful little baby girl, well, maybe this will be one holiday to remember!

I hope you all enjoy the final installment of The Rancher's Heirs. The Elliott brothers have been a joy to write!

Happy reading,

Jules

JULES BENNETT

A TEXAN FOR CHRISTMAS

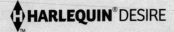

Recycling programs
for this product may
not exist in your area.

ISBN-13: 978-1-335-97186-9

A Texan for Christmas

Copyright © 2018 by Jules Bennett

Printed in U.S.A.

USA TODAY bestselling author **Jules Bennett** has published over sixty books and never tires of writing happy endings. Writing strong heroines and alpha heroes is Jules's favorite way to spend her workdays. Jules hosts weekly contests on her Facebook fan page and loves chatting with readers on Twitter, Facebook and via email through her website. Stay up-to-date by signing up for her newsletter at julesbennett.com.

Books by Jules Bennett

Harlequin Desire

What the Prince Wants
A Royal Amnesia Scandal
Maid for a Magnate
His Secret Baby Bombshell

Best Man Under the Mistletoe

The Rancher's Heirs

Twin Secrets
Claimed by the Rancher

Taming the Texan

A Texan for Christmas

Texas Cattleman's Club: Bachelor Auction

Most Eligible Texan

Visit her Author Profile page at Harlequin.com, or julesbennett.com, for more titles.

One

Scarlett Patterson clutched the handle of her small suitcase and waited.

And waited.

She'd knocked twice on the door, but still no answer. She knew this was the address she'd been given—a small cabin nestled in the back of the sprawling, picturesque Pebblebrook Ranch. She'd been told exactly who she'd be working for and her belly did flips just thinking of Beau Elliott—deemed Hollywood's Bad Boy, the Maverick of Movies, Cowboy Casanova…the titles were endless.

One thing was certain, if the tabloids were correct—he made no apologies about his affection for women. Scarlett wasn't sure she'd ever seen an image of him with the same woman.

That is, until his lover turned up pregnant. Then the two were spotted out together, but by then the rumors had begun—of drugs found in his lover's carry-on, of affairs started…or maybe they'd never stopped.

Why he'd come back home now, to this quiet town in Texas and his family's sprawling ranch, was none of her concern.

With a hand blocking her eyes from a rare glimpse of winter sun, Scarlett glanced around the open fields. Not a soul in sight. In the distance, a green field dotted with cattle stretched all the way to the horizon. This could easily be a postcard.

The Elliott land was vast. She'd heard there were several homes on the property and a portion of the place would soon become a dude ranch. In fact, this cabin would eventually be housing for guests of said dude ranch.

So why was Beau Elliott staying here instead of one of the main houses, with his brothers? Was he even planning to stick around?

So many mysteries…

But she wasn't here to inquire about his personal life and she certainly wouldn't be divulging any extra information about hers.

She was here to help his baby.

Even if that meant she had to come face-to-face with one of the sexiest men on the planet.

The snick of a lock had her turning her attention back around. When the door swung wide, it was all Scarlett could do to hold back her gasp.

Beau Elliott, Hollywood's baddest boy, stood before her sans shirt and wearing a pair of low-slung shorts. Scrolling ink went up one side of his waist, curling around well-defined pecs and disappearing over his shoulder.

Don't stare at the tattoos. Don't stare at the tattoos.

And, whatever you do, don't reach out to touch one.

"Who are you?"

The gravelly voice startled her back into reality. Scarlett realized she'd been staring.

Beau's broad frame filled the doorway, his stubbled jaw and bedhead indicating he hadn't had the best night. Apparently, according to the information she'd received, his last nanny had left last evening because of a family emergency.

Well, Scarlett wasn't having the best of days, either, so they were at least on a level playing field—other than the whole billionaire-peasant thing.

But she could use the extra money, so caring for an adorable five-month-old baby girl shouldn't be a problem, right?

Tamping down past hurts that threatened to creep up at the thought of caring for a child, Scarlett squared her shoulders and smiled. "I'm Scarlett Patterson. Your new nanny."

Beau blinked and gave her body a visual lick. "You're not old or frumpy," he growled.

Great. He'd already had some visual image in his head of who she should be. Maggie, the original nanny, was sweet as peach pie, but she *could* be best described as old and frumpy. Obviously, that was what Hollywood's Golden Child had thought he would be getting this morning, as well.

Beau Elliott, raised a rancher and then turned star of the screen, was going to be high maintenance. She could already tell.

Why would she expect anything less from someone who appeared to thrive on stardom and power?

Unfortunately, she knew that type all too well. Knew the type and ran like hell to avoid it.

She'd grown up with a man obsessed with money and getting what he wanted. Just when she thought she'd eliminated him from her life, he went on and became the governor. Scarlett was so over the power trip. Her stepfather and her mother weren't happy with her choices in life and had practically shunned her when they realized they couldn't control her. Which was fine. She'd rather do life on her own than be controlled...by anybody.

"Not old and frumpy. Is that a compliment or an observation?" She waved her hand to dismiss his answer before he could give her one. "Forget it. My looks and age are irrelevant. I am Maggie's replacement for the next three weeks."

"I requested someone like Maggie."

He still didn't make any attempt to move or to invite her inside. Even though this was Texas, the morning air chilled her.

Scarlett wasn't in the mood to deal with whatever hang-ups he had about nannies. Coming here after a year away from nanny duties was difficult enough. If she'd had her way, she would've found someone else to take this assignment, but the agency was short staffed.

This job was only for three weeks. Which meant she'd spend Christmas here, but the day after, she'd be heading to her new life in Dallas.

After the New Year, she'd start over fresh.

She could do this.

So why did she already feel the stirrings of a headache?

Oh, right. Because the once-dubbed "Sexiest Man Alive" was clearly used to getting his own way.

A bundle of nerves curled tightly in her belly. He might be sexy, but that didn't mean she had to put up with his attitude. Maybe he needed to remember that he was in a bind. He'd hired a nanny and Scarlett was it.

"Maggie, and everyone else at Nanny Poppins, is unavailable during the time frame you need."

Scarlett tried like hell to keep her professional smile in place—she did need this money, and she'd never leave a child without care. Plus, she wouldn't do a thing to tarnish the reputation of the company she'd worked for over the past several years.

She tipped her head and quirked a brow. "You do still need help, correct?"

Maggie had told Scarlett that Beau was brooding, that he kept to himself and only really came out of his shell when he interacted with his baby girl. That was all fine and good. Scarlett wasn't here to make friends or ogle the superstar, no matter how delicious he looked early in the morning.

A baby's cry pierced the awkward silence. With a muttered curse, Beau spun around and disappeared. Scarlett slowly stepped through the open door and shut it behind her.

Clearly the invitation wasn't going to happen.

"I feel so welcome," she muttered.

Scarlett leaned her suitcase against the wall and propped her small purse on top of it. The sounds of a fussy baby and Beau's deep, calming voice came from the bedroom to the right of the entryway.

As she took in the open floor plan of the cabin, she noted several things at once. Beau was either neat and tidy or he didn't have a lot of stuff. A pair of shiny new cowboy boots sat by the door and a black hat hung on a hook above the boots. The small kitchen had a drying rack with bottles on the counter and on the tiny table was a pink-and-white polka-dot bib.

She glanced to the left and noted another bedroom, the one she assumed would be hers, but she wasn't going to put her stuff in there just yet. Across the way, at the back of the cabin, was a set of patio doors that led to another porch. The area was cozy and perfect for the soon-to-be dude ranch.

The lack of Christmas decorations disturbed her, though. No tree, no stockings over the little fireplace, not even a wreath on the door. Who didn't want to celebrate Christmas? The most giving, joyous time of the year?

Christmas was absolutely her favorite holiday. Over the years she'd shared many Christmases with various families…all of which had been more loving and fulfilling than those of her stuffy, controlled childhood.

Scarlett continued to wait in the entryway, all while judging the Grinch's home. She didn't want to venture too far from the front door since he hadn't invited her in. It was obvious she wasn't what he'd expected, and he might ask her to leave.

Hopefully he wouldn't because she needed to work these three weeks. Those extra funds would go a long way toward helping her afford housing when she left Stone River to start her new life.

Even so, the next twenty-one days couldn't pass by fast enough.

Beau came back down the hall and Scarlett's heart tightened as a lump formed in her throat. A full assault on her emotions took over as knots in her stomach formed.

She couldn't do this. No matter how short the time span, she couldn't stay with this man, in this confined space, caring for his daughter for three weeks and not come out unscathed.

She wasn't sure which sight hit her hardest—the well-sculpted shirtless man or the baby he was holding.

Being this close to the little girl nearly brought her to her knees. Scarlett knew coming back as a hands-on nanny would be difficult, but she hadn't fully prepared herself for just how hard a hit her heart would take.

She'd purposely given up working in homes only a year ago. She'd requested work in the office, even though the administrative side paid less than round-the-clock nanny services. She'd been Nanny Poppins's most sought-after employee for eight years, but after everything that had happened, her boss completely understood Scarlett's need to distance herself from babies and families.

Fate had been cruel, stealing her chance of having kids of her own. She wasn't sure she was ready to see another parent have what she wanted. Working for Beau Elliott would be difficult to say the least, but Scarlett would push through and then she could move on. One last job. She could do this…she hoped.

The sweet baby continued to fuss, rubbing her eyes and sniffling. No doubt she was tired. From the looks of both of them, they'd had a long night.

Instinct had Scarlett reaching out and taking the baby, careful not to brush her fingertips against the hard planes of Beau's bare chest.

Well, she had to assume they were hard because she'd stared at them for a solid two minutes.

The second that sweet baby smell hit Scarlett, she nearly lost it. Her eyes burned, her throat tightened. But the baby's needs had to come first. That's why Scarlett was here. Well, that and to get double the pay so she could finally move to Dallas.

She could've turned down this job, but Maggie was in a bind, the company was in a bind, and they'd been so good to Scarlett since she'd started working there.

Scarlett simply couldn't say no.

"Oh, sweetheart, it's okay."

She patted the little girl's back and swayed slowly. Maggie had told her the baby was a joy to be around.

"Madelyn."

Scarlett blinked. "Excuse me?"

"Her name is Madelyn."

Well, at least they were getting somewhere and he wasn't ready to push her out the door. Scarlett already knew Madelyn's name and had read all the pertinent information regarding this job, but it was nice that Beau wasn't growling at her anymore.

Still, she wished he'd go put a shirt on. She couldn't keep her eyes completely off him, not when he was on display like that. Damn man probably thought he could charm her or distract her by flexing all those glorious, delicious muscles. Muscles that would no doubt feel taut beneath her touch.

Scarlett swallowed and blinked away the erotic

image before she could take it too far. At least she had something else to think of other than her own gut-clenching angst and baby fever. Hunky heart-throb to the rescue.

Scarlett turned away from the distracting view of her temporary boss and walked toward the tiny living area. The room seemed a little larger thanks to the patio doors leading onto the covered porch, which was decorated with a cute table and chair set.

The whole cabin was rather small, but it wasn't her place to ask why a billionaire film star lived in this cramped space on his family's estate. None of her business. This would just be a quick three weeks in December—in and out—in the most un-festive place ever.

Maybe she could sneak in some Christmas here and there. Every child deserved some twinkle lights or a stocking, for heaven's sake. Definitely a tree. Without it, where would Santa put the presents?

"She's been cranky all night," Beau said behind her. "I've tried everything, but I can't make her happy. I've never had that happen before."

The frustration in his voice softened Scarlett a bit. Beau might be a womanizer and a party animal, if the tabloids were right—which would explain his comfort level with wearing no shirt—but he obviously cared for his daughter.

Scarlett couldn't help but wonder where the mother was, but again, it was none of her concern. She'd seen enough tabloid stories to figure the mother was likely in rehab or desperately needing to be there.

Madelyn let out a wail, complete with tears and everything. The poor baby was miserable, which now made three of them, all under the same roof.

Let the countdown to her move begin.

How the hell had his nanny situation gone from Mrs. Doubtfire to Miss December?

The sultry vixen with rich skin, deep brown eyes, and silky black hair was too striking. But it was those curves in all the right places that had definitely woken him up this morning. His entire body had been ready to stand at attention, so perhaps he'd come across a little gruff.

But, damn it, he had good reason.

He'd been assured a replacement nanny would arrive bright and early, but he'd expected the agency to send another grandmother type.

Where was the one with a thick middle, elastic pants, sensible shoes and a gray bun? Where the hell did he order up another one of those? Warts would help, too. False teeth, even.

Beau stood back as he watched Scarlett comfort his daughter.

Scarlett. Of course she'd have a sultry name to match everything else sultry about her.

Not too long ago she would've been exactly his type. He would've wasted no time in charming and seducing her. But now his entire life had changed and the only woman he had time for was the sweet five-month-old he'd saved from the clutches of her partying, strung-out mother.

Money wasn't something he cared about—perhaps because he'd always had it—but it sure as hell came in handy. Like when he needed to pay off his ex so he could have Madelyn. Jennifer had selfishly taken the money, signed over the rights, and had nearly skipped out of their lives and onto the next star she thought would catapult her career.

The fact that he'd been used by her wasn't even relevant. He could care less about how he'd been treated, but he would not have their baby act as a pawn for Jennifer's own vindictive nature.

Beau couldn't get Madelyn out of Hollywood fast enough. His daughter was not going to be brought up in the lifestyle that too many fell into—himself included.

He'd overcome his past and the ugliness that surrounded his life when he'd first gotten into LA. He'd worked damn hard and was proud of the life he had built, but now his focus had to shift and changes needed to be made.

Coming home hadn't been ideal because he knew exactly the type of welcome he'd get. But there was nowhere else he wanted to be right now. He needed his family, even if he took hell from Colt, Hayes and Nolan for showing up after years of being away… with a kid in tow.

Thankfully, his brothers and their women all

doted over Madelyn. That's all he wanted. No matter how people treated him or ignored him, Beau wanted his daughter to be surrounded with love.

His life was a mess, his future unknown. Hell, he couldn't think past today. He had a movie premiere two days before Christmas and he'd have to go, but other than that, he had no clue.

All that mattered was Madelyn, making sure she had a solid foundation and family that loved her. The calls from his new agent didn't matter, the movie premiere didn't matter, all the press he was expected to do to promote the film sure as hell didn't matter. To say he was burned out would be a vast understatement.

Beau needed some space to think and the calming serenity of Pebblebrook Ranch provided just that.

Unfortunately, concentrating would be rather difficult with a centerfold look-alike staying under his roof. Well, not his roof exactly. He was only using one of the small cabins on the land until the dude ranch officially opened in a few months. His father's dream was finally coming to fruition.

Beau wondered how he'd come to this moment of needing someone. He prided himself on never needing anyone. He had homes around the globe, cars that would make any man weep with envy, even his own private island, but the one place he wanted and needed to be was right here with his family—whether they wanted him here or not.

Beau had turned his back on this land and his

family years ago. That was the absolute last thing he'd intended to do, but he'd gotten swept away into the fortune and fame. Eventually days had rolled into months, then into years, and the time had passed too quickly.

But now he was back home, and as angry as his brothers were, they'd given him a place to stay. Temporary, but at least it was something. He knew it was only because he had Madelyn, but he'd take it.

"She's teething."

Beau pulled his thoughts from his family drama and focused on the nanny. "Teething? She's only five months old."

Scarlett continued to sway back and forth with Madelyn in her arms. His sweet girl sucked on her fist and alternated between sniffles and cries. At least the screaming wasn't so constant like last night. Having his daughter so upset and him feeling so helpless had absolutely gutted him. He would've done anything to help her, but he'd been clueless. He'd spent the night questioning just how good of a father he really was.

Madelyn's wide, dark eyes stared up at the new nanny as if trying to figure out where the stranger had come from.

He was having a difficult time not staring, as well, and he knew full well where she came from—every single one of his erotic fantasies.

"Her gums are swollen and she's drooling quite a bit," Scarlett stated. "All perfectly normal. Do you happen to have any cold teething rings in your fridge?"

Cold teething rings? What the hell was that? He was well stocked with formula and bottles, diapers and wipes, but rings in the fridge? Nope.

He had an app that told him what babies should be doing and what they needed at different stages, but the rings hadn't been mentioned yet.

"I'm guessing no from the look on your face." Scarlett went into the kitchen area and opened the freezer. "Can you get me a napkin or towel?"

Beau wasn't used to taking orders, but he'd do anything to bring his daughter some comfort. He grabbed a clean dishcloth from the counter and handed it to her. He watched as she held on to the ice through the cloth and rubbed it on his daughter's gums. After a few minutes the fussing grew quieter until she finally stopped.

"I'll get some teething rings today," Scarlett murmured as if talking to herself more than him. "They are wonderful for instant relief. If you have any children's pain reliever, we can also rub that on her gums, but I try natural approaches before I go to medicine."

Okay, so maybe Miss December was going to be an asset. He liked that she offered natural options for Madelyn's care. He also liked that she seemed to be completely unimpressed with his celebrity status. Something about that was so refreshing and even more attractive.

Watch it. You already got in trouble with one sexy woman. She's the nanny, not the next bedmate.

He told himself he didn't need the silent warning that rang in his head. Scarlett Patterson would only be here until the day after Christmas. Surely he could keep his libido in control for that long. It wasn't like he had the time anyway. He couldn't smooth the ruffled feathers of his family, care for his child and seduce a woman all before December 26.

No matter how sexy the new nanny was.

Besides, he thought, it couldn't get more clichéd than that—the movie star and the nanny. How many of those stories had he read in the tabloids of late?

No, there was no way he was going to make a move on the woman who was saving his sanity and calming his baby. Besides, he respected women; his mother had raised Southern gentlemen, after all. The media liked to report that he rolled out of one woman's bed and right into another, but he wasn't quite that popular. Not to mention, any woman he'd ever been with had known he wasn't looking for long-term—and agreed with it.

Beau had a feeling Scarlett would be a long-term type of girl. She likely had a family—or maybe she didn't. If this was her full-time job, she probably didn't have time to take care of a family.

Honestly, he shouldn't be letting his mind wander into the territory of Scarlett's personal life. She was his nanny, nothing more.

But damn it, did she have to look so good in her

little pink capris and white sleeveless button-up? Didn't she have a uniform? Something up to her neck, down to her ankles and with sleeves? Even if she was completely covered up, she still had those expressive, doe-like eyes, a perfectly shaped mouth and adorable dimples.

Damn it. He should not be noticing each little detail of his new nanny.

"Why don't you go rest?" Scarlett suggested, breaking into his erotic thoughts. "I can take care of her. You look like hell."

Beau stared across the narrow space for a half second before he found his voice. Nobody talked to him like that except his brothers, and even that had been years ago.

"Are you always that blunt with your clients?"

"I try to be honest at all times," she replied sweetly. "I can't be much help to you if you just want me here to boost your ego and lie to your face."

Well, that was a rarity…if she was even telling the truth now. Beau hadn't met a woman who was honest and genuine. Nearly everyone he'd met was out for herself and to hell with anyone around them. And money. They always wanted money.

Another reason he needed the simplicity of Pebblebrook. He just wanted to come back to his roots, to decompress and figure out what the hell to do with his life now. He wanted the open spaces, wanted to see the blue skies without buildings blocking the view. And he needed to mend the relationships he'd left behind. What better time than Christmas?

"I'm Beau." When she drew her brows in, he went on. "I didn't introduce myself before."

"I'm aware of who you are."

He waited for her to say something else, but clearly she'd formed an opinion of him and didn't want to share. Fine. So long as she kept his daughter comfortable and helped him until Maggie returned, he could care less what she thought.

But she'd have to get in line because his brothers had already dubbed him the prodigal son and were eager to put him in his place. Nothing less than he deserved, he reasoned.

As he watched Scarlett take over the care of Madelyn, Beau knew this was what he deserved, too. A sexy-as-hell woman as his nanny. This was his penance for the bastard he'd been over the past several years.

He'd do well to remember he was a new man now. He'd do well to remember she was here for his daughter, not for his personal pleasure. He'd also do well to remember he had more important things to do than drop Scarlett Patterson into each and every one of his fantasies…even if she would make the perfect lead.

Two

Madelyn had calmed down and was now settled in her crib napping. There was a crib in each of the two bedrooms, but Scarlett opted to put Madelyn in the room Maggie had vacated. This would be Scarlett's room now and she simply didn't think going into Beau's was a smart idea.

After she'd put her luggage and purse in her room, Beau had given her a very brief tour of the cabin, so she'd gotten a glimpse into his personal space. The crib in his room had been nestled next to the king-size bed. Scarlett tried not to, but the second she recalled those messed sheets, she procured an image of him lying there in a pair of snug boxer briefs... or nothing at all.

Scarlett groaned and gently shut the bedroom door, careful not to let the latch snick. She wasn't sure how light of a sleeper Madelyn was, so until she got to know the sweet bundle a little better—

But she couldn't get to know her too much, could she? There wasn't going to be time, and for Scarlett's sanity and heart, she had to keep an emotional distance. Giving herself that pep talk and actually doing it were two totally different things.

Before her surgery, she'd thrown herself into each and every job. Before her surgery, she'd always felt like one unit with the families she worked with.

Before her surgery, she'd had dreams.

The hard knot in her chest never eased. Whether she thought of what she'd lost or was just doing day-to-day things, the ache remained a constant reminder.

Scarlett stepped back into the living area and found Beau standing at the patio doors, his back to her. At least he'd put a T-shirt on. Even so, he filled it out, stretching the material over those chiseled muscles she'd seen firsthand. Clothes or no clothes, the image had been burned into her memory bank and there was no erasing it.

"Madelyn's asleep," she stated.

Beau threw her a glance over his shoulder, then turned his attention back to the view of the open field.

Okay. Clearly he wasn't chatty. Fine by her. He must be a lonely, miserable man. She'd always wondered if celebrities were happy. After all, money certainly couldn't buy everything. Her stepfather was proof of that. He'd been a state representative for years before moving up to governor. He'd wanted his children—he included her in that mix—to all enter the political arena so they would be seen as a powerhouse family.

Thanks, but no thanks. She preferred a simpler life—or at least one without lies, deceit, fake smiles and cheesy campaign slogans.

"If there's something you need to go do, I'll be here," she told Beau. Not surprisingly, he didn't answer. Maybe he gave a grunt, but she couldn't tell if that was a response or just indigestion.

Scarlett turned toward the kitchen to take stock of what type of formula and baby things Madelyn used. Being here a short time, she wanted to make sure the transitions between Maggie and her then back to Maggie went smoothly. Regardless of what Scarlett thought of Beau, Madelyn was the only one here who mattered.

Before Scarlett could step into the kitchen, a knock sounded on the front door.

Beau shifted, his gaze landing on the closed door. He looked like he'd rather run in the opposite direction than face whoever was on the other side. Given that they were on private property, likely the guest was just his family, so what was the issue? Wasn't that why he'd come home? To be with his family for the holidays?

When he made no attempt to move, Scarlett asked, "Should I get that?"

He gave a curt nod and Scarlett reached for the knob. The second she opened the door, she gasped.

Sweet mercy. There were two of them. Another Beau stood before her, only this one was clean shaven and didn't have the scowl. But those shoulders and dark eyes were dead on and just as potent to her heart rate.

"Ma'am," the Beau look-alike said with a drawl and a tip of his black cowboy hat. "I'm Colt Elliott, Beau's twin. You must be the replacement nanny."

Another Elliott and a *twin*. Mercy sakes, this job was not going to be a hardship whatsoever if she had to look at these men each day.

She knew there were four Elliott sons, but wow. Nobody warned her they were clones. Now she wondered if the other two would stop by soon. One could hope.

"Yes," she said when she realized he was waiting on her to respond to his question. "I'm Scarlett."

Colt's dark eyes went from her to Beau. "Is this a bad time?"

Scarlett stepped back. "Not at all. I just got the baby to sleep. I can wait outside while you two talk. It's a beautiful day."

She turned and caught Beau's gaze on her. Did he always have that dramatic, heavy-lidded, movie-star stare? Did he ever turn off the act or was that mysterious, sexy persona natural?

"If you'll excuse me." She turned to Colt. "It was a pleasure meeting you."

"Pleasure was mine, ma'am."

Somehow Scarlett managed to get out the front door without tripping over her own two feet, because that sexy, low Southern drawl those Elliott boys had was rather knee-weakening.

Once she made it to the porch, she walked to the wooden swing on the end in front of her bedroom window. She sank down onto the seat and let the gentle breeze cool off her heated body. December in Texas wasn't too hot, wasn't too cold. In this part of the state, the holiday weather was always perfect. Though the evenings and nights could get chilly.

Good thing there were fireplaces in this cabin. Fireplaces that could lead one to instantly think of romantic talks and shedding of clothes, being wrapped in a blanket in the arms of a strong man.

Scarlett shut her eyes as she rested her feet on the porch and stopped the swaying swing. There would be no romance and no fires…at least not the passionate kind.

Raised voices filtered from inside. Clearly the Elliott twins were not happy with each other. Two sexy-as-hell alphas going at it sounded like every woman's fantasy, but she couldn't exactly barge in and interrupt.

Then she heard it. The faint cry from her bedroom, right on the other side of the window from where she sat. Well, damn it.

Scarlett pushed off the swing and jerked open the front door. Hot men or not, powerful men or not, she didn't take kindly to anyone disturbing a sleeping baby.

As she marched toward her bedroom, she shot a warning glare in the direction of the guys, who were now practically chest to chest. She didn't have time to worry about their issues, not when Madelyn had barely been asleep twenty minutes.

Scarlett crossed to the crib and gently picked up the sweet girl. After grabbing her fuzzy yellow blanket, Scarlett sank into the nearby rocking chair and patted Madelyn's bottom to calm her.

Madelyn's little sniffles and heavy lids were Scarlett's main focus right now. She eased the chair into a gentle motion with her foot and started humming "You Are My Sunshine." Madelyn didn't take long to nestle back into sleep and Scarlett's heart clenched. She'd just hold her a tad longer… It had been so long since she'd rocked a little one.

She had no idea what happened with Beau and the baby's mother, but the tabloids and social media had been abuzz with a variety of rumors over the past few weeks.

Well, actually, the couple had been quite the fodder for gossip a lot longer. It was over a year ago when they were first spotted half naked on a beach in Belize. Then the pregnancy seemed to send shock waves through the media. Of course, after the baby was born, there was all that speculation on the state of the mother and she was seen less and less.

Chatter swirled about her cheating, then her rehab, then the breakup.

Then there was talk of Beau. One online source stated he'd been passed over for a part in an epic upcoming blockbuster. One said he'd had a fight with his new agent. Another reported that he and his ex had been spotted arguing at a party and one or both had been inebriated.

Honestly, Beau Elliott was a complication she didn't want to get tangled with, so whatever happened to send him rushing home was his problem. That didn't mean, however, that a child should have to suffer for the sins of the parents.

Once Madelyn was good and asleep, Scarlett put her down in the crib. There was a light tap on the door moments before it eased open.

Scarlett turned from the sleeping baby to see Beau filling the doorway.

"Is she asleep again?" he whispered.

Stepping away from the crib, Scarlett nodded. "Next time you want to have a family fight, take it outside."

His eyes darkened. "This isn't your house," he stated, taking a step closer to her.

Scarlett stood at the edge of the bed and crossed her arms. "It isn't exactly your house, either," she retorted. "But Madelyn is my job now and I won't have her disturbed when she's been fussy and obviously needs sleep. Maybe if you put her needs first—"

In a second, Beau had closed the gap and was all but leaning over her, so close that she had to hold on to the bedpost to stay upright.

"Every single thing I do is putting her needs first," he growled through gritted teeth. "You've been here less than two hours, so don't even presume to know what's going on."

Scarlett placed her hand on his chest to get him to ease back, but the heat from his body warmed her in a way she couldn't explain…and shouldn't dwell on.

She jerked her hand back and glanced away, only to have her eyes land on the pile of lacy panties she'd thrown on her bed when she'd started unpacking earlier.

There went more of that warmth spreading through her. What were the odds Beau hadn't noticed?

She risked glancing back at him, but…nope. He'd noticed all right. His eyes were fixed on her unmentionables.

Beau cleared his throat and raked a hand over the back of his neck before glancing to where his baby slept peacefully in the crib on the other side of the room.

When his dark eyes darted back to her, they pinned her in place. "We need to talk." Then he turned and marched out, likely expecting her to follow.

Scarlett closed her eyes and pulled in a breath as she attempted to count backward from ten. This was only the first day. She knew there would be some bumps in the road, right?

She just didn't expect those bumps to be the chills rushing over her skin from the brief yet toe-curling contact she'd just had with her employer.

Beau ground his molars and clenched his fists at his sides. It had been quite a while since he'd been with a woman and the one currently staying under his roof was driving him absolutely insane…and it wasn't even lunchtime on her first day of employment.

Those damn panties. All that lace, satin…strings. Mercy, he couldn't get the image out of his head. Never once did he think his nanny's underwear would cause his brain to fry, but here he was with a silent seductress helping to take care of his daughter and he couldn't focus. Likely she didn't even have a clue how she was messing with his hormones.

Scarlett honestly did have Madelyn's best interest in mind. She was none too happy with him and Colt earlier and he wasn't too thrilled with the situation, either. Of all the people angry with him for his actions and for being away from home so long, Colt was by far the most furious. Ironic, he thought. He'd figure his own twin would try to have a little compassion.

Unfortunately, there was so much more contention between them than just the missing years. Coming home at Christmas and thinking things would be magical and easily patched up had been completely naive on his part. But damn it, he'd been hopeful. They'd been the best of friends once, with a twin bond that was stronger than anything he'd ever known.

Delicate footsteps slid across the hardwood floor, interrupting his thoughts. Beau shored up his mental strength and turned to face Scarlett. Why did she have to look like a walking dream? That curvy body, the dark eyes, her flawless dark skin and black hair that gave the illusion of silk sliding down her back.

Damn those panties. Now when he saw her he wondered what she wore underneath her clothes. Lace or satin? Pink or yellow?

"What do you want to talk about?" she asked, making no move to come farther into the living area.

Beau gestured toward the oversize sectional sofa. "Have a seat."

She eyed him for a moment before finally crossing the room and sitting down on the end of the couch. She crossed her ankles and clasped her hands as if she were in some business meeting with a CEO.

Beau stood next to her. "Relax."

"I'd relax more if you weren't looming over me."

Part of him wanted to laugh. Most women would love for him to "loom" over them. Hell, most women would love him under them, as well. Perhaps that's why he found Scarlett of the silky panties so intriguing. She truly didn't care that he was an A-list actor with more money than he could ever spend and the power to obtain nearly anything he ever wanted.

Beau didn't want to make her uncomfortable and it certainly wasn't his intention to be a jerk. It pained him to admit it, but he needed her. He was only a few weeks out on his own with Madelyn and he really didn't want to screw up this full-time parenting job. This would be the most important job he'd ever have.

"We probably need to set some rules here," he started.

Rules like keeping all underwear hidden in a drawer at all times. Oh, and maybe if she could get some long pants and high-neck shirts, that would certainly help. Wouldn't it?

Maggie sat straighter. "I work for you, Mr. Elliott. Just tell me the rules you had for Maggie."

Beau nearly snorted. Rules for Maggie were simple: help with Madelyn while Beau was out working on the ranch and trying to figure his life out. The rules for Scarlett? They'd go beyond not leaving your lingerie out. He mentally added a few more: stop looking so damn innocent and sexy at the same time, stop with the defiant chin that he wanted to nip at and work his way down.

But of course he couldn't voice those rules. He cleared his throat and instead of enumerating his expectations, he took a different approach.

"I'm a hands-on dad." He started with that because that was the most important. "Madelyn is my life. I'm only going to be at Pebblebrook for a short time, but while I'm here, I plan on getting back to my roots and helping to get this dude ranch up and running."

That is, if his brothers would let him in on realizing their father's dream. That was still a heated debate, especially since Beau hadn't been to see Grant Elliott yet.

His father had been residing in an assisted-living facility for the past few years. The bad blood between them couldn't be erased just because Beau had made a deathbed promise to the one man who had been more like a father to him than his real one.

Still, Beau was man enough to admit that he was afraid to see his dad. What if his dad didn't recognize him? Grant had been diagnosed with dementia and lately, more often than not, he didn't know his own children. Even the sons who'd been around the past few years. Beau wasn't sure he was strong enough to face that reality just yet.

"Beau?"

Scarlett's soft tone pulled him out of his thoughts. Where was he? Right, the rules.

"Yeah, um. I can get up with Madelyn during the night. I didn't hire a nanny so I could be lazy and just pass her care off. I prefer a live-in nanny more because I'm still…"

"Nervous?" she finished with raised brows. "It's understandable. Most first-time parents are. Babies are pretty easy, though. They'll pretty much tell you what's wrong, you know, just not with actual words."

No, he actually didn't know. He just knew when Madelyn cried he wanted her to stop because he didn't want her unhappy.

Beau had spent the past five months fighting with his ex, but she'd only wanted Madelyn as a bargaining chip. He'd finally gotten his lawyer to really tighten the screws and ultimately, Jennifer James—wannabe actress and worthless mother— signed away her parental rights.

As much as he hated the idea of Madelyn not having a mother around, his daughter was better off.

Beau studied his new, refreshing nanny. "I assume you don't have children since you're a nanny full-time."

Some emotion slid right over her, taking away that sweet, calm look she'd had since she'd arrived. He could swear an invisible shield slid right between them. Her lips thinned, her head tipped up a notch and her eyes were completely unblinking.

"No children," she said succinctly.

There was backstory behind that simple statement. He knew that for sure. And he was curious.

"Yet you know so much about them," he went on. "Do you want a family of your own one day?"

"My personal life is none of your concern. That's my number-one rule that you can add to your list."

Why the hell had he even asked? He didn't need to know her on a deeper level, but now that she'd flat-out refused to go there, he wanted to find out every last secret she kept hidden. He hadn't asked Maggie personal questions, but then Maggie hadn't pulled up emotions in him like this, either.

Even though he'd just vowed to stay out of Scarlett's personal business, well, he couldn't help himself. If she was just standoffish, that would be one thing, but hurt and vulnerability had laced her tone. He was a sucker for a woman in need.

Scarlett, though, clearly didn't want to be the topic of conversation, something he not only understood but respected. He told himself he should focus on his purpose for being back home and not worry about what his temporary nanny did in her off time.

Beau nodded in affirmation at her demand. "Very well. These three weeks shouldn't be a problem, then."

He came to his feet, most likely to get away from the lie he'd just settled between them. Truthfully, everything about having her here was a problem, but that was on him. Apparently she didn't care that his hormones had chosen now to stand up and pay attention to her. She also didn't seem to care who he was. He was just another client and his celebrity status didn't do a damn thing for her.

While he appreciated her not throwing herself at him, his ego wasn't so quick to accept the hit. This was all new territory for him where a beautiful woman was concerned.

"I'm going to change and head to the main stable

for a bit." He pulled his cell from his pocket. "Give me your cell number and I'll text you so you have my number. If you need anything at all, message me and I'll be right back."

Once the numbers were exchanged, Beau picked up his boots by the front door and went to his room to change. He slipped on a pair of comfortable old jeans, but the boots were new and needed to be broken in. He'd had to buy another pair when he came back. The moment he'd left Pebblebrook years ago, he'd ditched any semblance of home.

Odd how he couldn't wait to dig right back in. The moment he'd turned into the long white-fence-lined drive, he'd gotten that kick of nostalgia as memories of working side by side with his brothers and his father came flooding back.

Right now he needed to muck some stalls to clear his head and take his mind off the most appealing woman he'd encountered in a long time…maybe ever.

But he doubted even grunt work would help. Because at the end of the day, he'd still come back here where she would be wearing her lacy lingerie…and where they would be spending their nights all alone with only an infant as their chaperone.

Three

"You're going to get your pretty new boots scuffed."

Beau turned toward the open end of the stable. His older brother Hayes stood with his arms crossed over his chest, his tattoos peeking from beneath the hems of the sleeves on his biceps.

"I need to break them in," Beau replied, instinctively glancing down to the shiny steel across the point on the toe.

If anyone knew about coming home, it was Hayes. Beau's ex-soldier brother had been overseas fighting in Afghanistan and had seen some serious action that had turned Hayes into an entirely different man than the one Beau remembered.

Whatever had happened to his brother had hardened him, but he was back at the ranch with the love of his life and raising a little boy that he'd taken in as his own. He'd found a happy ending. Beau wasn't so sure that would ever happen for him—or even if he wanted it to.

"So, what? You're going to try to get back into the ranching life?" Hayes asked as he moved to grab a pitchfork hanging on the inside of the tack room. "Or are we just a stepping stone?"

Beau didn't know what the hell he was going to do. He knew in less than three weeks he had a movie debut he had to attend, but beyond that, he'd been dodging his new agent's calls because there was no way Beau was ready to look at another script just yet. His focus was needed elsewhere.

Like on his daughter.

On his future.

"Right now I'm just trying to figure out where the hell to go." Beau gripped his own pitchfork and glanced to the stall with Doc inside. "Nolan ever come and help?"

Hayes headed toward the other end of the row. "When he can. He stays busy at the hospital, but he's cut his hours since marrying and having a kid of his own. His priorities have shifted."

Not just Nolan's priorities, but also Colt's and Hayes's. All three of his brothers had fallen in love and were enjoying their ready-made families.

Beau had been shocked when he'd pulled into the

drive and seen his brothers standing on Colt's sprawling front porch with three ladies he didn't know and
four children. The ranch had apparently exploded
into the next generation while he'd been gone.

Beau worked around Nolan's stallion and put fresh
straw in the stall before moving to the next one. For
the next hour he and Hayes worked together just
like when they'd been kids. Teamwork on the ranch
had been important to their father. He'd instilled a
set of ethics in his boys that no formal education
could match.

Of course they had ranch hands, but there was
something about getting back to your roots, Beau
knew, that did some sort of reset to your mental
health. At this point he needed to try anything to
help him figure out what his next move should be.

He actually enjoyed manual labor. Even as a kid
and a teen, he'd liked working alongside his father
and brothers. But over time, Beau had gotten the urge
to see the world, to find out if there was more to life
than ranching, and learning how to turn one of the
toughest professions into a billion-dollar lifestyle.
The idea of being in charge of Pebblebrook once his
father retired held no shred of interest to Beau. He
knew Colt had always wanted that position so why
would Beau even attempt to share it?

"So you all live here on the estate?" Beau asked
when he and Hayes had completed their stalls and
met in the middle of the barn.

Hayes rested his hand on the top of the pitchfork

handle and swiped his other forearm across his damp forehead. "Yeah. I renovated Granddad's old house back by the fork in the river and the creek. I've always loved that place and it just seemed logical when I came back."

The original farmhouse for Pebblebrook would be the perfect home for Hayes and his family, providing privacy, but still remaining on Elliott land.

When they'd all been boys they'd ventured to the back of the property on their horses or ATVs and used it as a giant getaway or a man cave. They'd had the ultimate fort and pretended to be soldiers or cowboys in the Old West.

Once upon a time the Elliott brothers were all close, inseparable. But now...

Beau was virtually starting over with his own family. That deathbed promise to his former agent was so much more difficult to execute than he'd originally thought. But Hector had made Beau vow he'd go home and mend fences. At the time Beau had agreed, but now he knew saying the words had been the easy part.

He leaned back against Doc's stall and stared blankly.

"Hey." Hayes studied Beau before slapping a large hand over his shoulder. "It's going to take some time. Nolan is hurt, but he's not pissed. Me? I'm just glad you're here, though I wonder if you'll stay. So I guess that makes me cautious. But Colt, well, he's pissed and hurt, so that's the one you need to be careful with."

Beau snorted and shook his head. "Yeah, we've already had words."

Like when Colt swung by earlier to talk, but ended up going off because of the new nanny. Colt claimed Beau was still a wild child and a player, hiring a nanny looking like that. Beau had prayed Scarlett hadn't heard Colt's accusations. She was a professional and he didn't want her disrespected or made to feel unwelcome. Not that his brother was disrespecting Scarlett. No, he was aiming that all at Beau.

Even if the choice had been his, Beau sure as hell wouldn't have chosen a woman who looked like Scarlett to spend twenty-four hours a day with inside that small cabin. Even he wasn't that much of a masochist.

Beau had no idea what had originally brought Colt over to see him, but he had a feeling their morning talk wasn't the last of their heated debates.

"You'd think my twin would be the most understanding," Beau muttered.

"Not when he's the one who held this place together once Dad couldn't," Hayes retorted. "I was overseas, Nolan was married to his surgery schedule and you were gone. Colt's always wanted this life. Ranching was it for him, so I guess the fact you wanted nothing to do with it only made the hurt worse. Especially when you rarely called or came back to visit."

Beau knew coming back would rip his heart open, but he'd had no clue his brother would just continually pour salt into the wound. But he had nobody to blame but himself. He was man enough to take it, though. He would push through the hard times and reconnect with his family. If losing Hector had taught him anything, it was that time was fleeting.

"I can't make up for the past," Beau started. "And I can't guarantee I'll stay forever. I just needed somewhere to bring Madelyn, and home seemed like the most logical place. I don't care how I'm treated, just as long as she's loved. I can work on Colt and hopefully mend that relationship."

"Maybe you should start with seeing Dad if you want to try to make amends with anyone."

The heavy dose of guilt he'd been carrying around for some time grew weightier at Hayes's statement. His older brother was absolutely right, yet fear had kept Beau from reaching out to his father since he'd been home.

"Will he even know me?" Beau asked, almost afraid of the answer.

Hayes shrugged. "Maybe not, but what matters is that you're there."

Beau swallowed the lump of emotions. Everything he'd heard over the past year was that their father barely knew anything anymore. The Alzheimer's had trapped him inside his mind. He and Beau may have had major differences in the past, but Grant Elliott was still his father and Beau respected the hell out of that man…though he hadn't done a great job of showing it over the years.

His father had been a second-generation rancher and took pride in his work. He'd wanted his sons to follow in that same path of devotion. Beau, though, had been a rebellious teen with wandering feet and a chip on his shoulder. Pebblebrook hadn't been enough to contain him and he'd moved away. On his own for the first time, he'd wanted to experience everything that had been denied him back home, and ended up in trouble. Then he was discovered and dubbed "a natural" after a ridiculous commercial he wanted to forget.

Beau threw himself into the acting scene hard. His career had seemed to skyrocket overnight.

At first he'd been on a path to destruction, then a path to stardom. And through it all, he hadn't even thought of coming home. He'd been too wrapped up in himself. No excuses.

Then one day he'd realized how much time had passed. He had come home but the cold welcome he'd received had sent him straight back to LA.

But this time was different. This time he was going to stay, at least through the holidays, no matter how difficult it might be.

"I'll go see him," Beau promised, finally meeting Hayes's eyes. "I'm just not ready."

"Always making excuses."

Beau and Hayes turned to the sound of Colt's angry voice. Just what he needed, another round with his pissed brother.

* * *

Colt glanced to the pitchfork in Beau's hand. "Are you practicing for a part or actually attempting to help?"

"Colt—"

"No." Beau held out his hand, cutting Hayes off. "It's not your fight."

Hayes nodded and took Beau's pitchfork and his own back to the tack room, giving Beau and Colt some privacy.

"I came home because I needed somewhere safe to bring my daughter," Beau stated, that chip on his shoulder more evident than ever. "I came home because it was time and I'd hoped we could put aside our differences for Christmas."

Did he think he could just waltz back onto the ranch and sing carols around the Christmas tree and all would be well? Had he been gone so long that he could just ignore the tension and the hurt that resided here?

"You won't find a red-carpet welcome here," Colt grunted. "We've gotten along just fine without you for years. So if you're just going to turn around and leave again, don't bother with all this show now. Christmas is a busy time for Annabelle at the B and B. I don't have time to figure out what the hell you're doing or not doing."

Seeing his twin back here where they'd shared so many memories…

Every part of Colt wished this was a warm family reunion, but the reality was quite different.

Beau had chosen to stay away, to make a new family, a new life amidst all the Hollywood hoopla, the parties, the women, the money and jet-setting.

Bitterness had settled into Colt long ago and showed no sign of leaving.

"What did you want when you came by this morning?" Beau asked. "Other than to berate me."

Hayes carried a blanket and saddle down the stable and passed them, obviously trying to get the hell out of here and not intervene.

Colt hooked his thumbs through his belt loops. "I was going to give you a chance to explain. Annabelle told me I should hear your side, but then I saw your replacement nanny and realized nothing about you has changed."

Of course Beau would have a stunning woman living under his roof with the guise of being a nanny. Was his brother ever going to mature and just own up to his responsibilities?

"Replacement nanny?" Hayes chimed up.

Beau's eyes narrowed—apparently Colt had hit a nerve. But they both ignored Hayes's question.

The resentment and turmoil that had been bubbling and brewing over the years was best left between him and his twin. Colt didn't want to drag anybody else into this mix.

Though his wife had already wedged herself into the drama. He knew she meant well, he knew she wanted one big happy family, especially considering she lost her only sibling too early in life. But still, there was so much pain in the past that had only grown like a tumor over the years. Some things simply couldn't be fixed.

Beau kept his gaze straight ahead to Colt. "Who I have helping with Madelyn is none of your concern and I didn't decide who the agency sent to replace Maggie. Her husband fell and broke his hip so she had to go care for him for a few weeks until their daughter can come help. If you have a problem, maybe you'd like to apply for the job."

"Maybe you could worry more about your daughter and less about your dick—"

Beau didn't think before his fist planted in the side of Colt's jaw. He simply reacted. But before he could land a second shot, a restraining hand stopped him. Hayes stood between the brothers, his hands on each of their chests.

"All right, we're not doing this," Hayes told them both.

"Looks like I missed the official work reunion."

At the sound of the new voice, Beau turned to see Nolan come striding in. No fancy doctor clothes for his oldest brother. Nolan looked like the rest of them with his jeans and Western shirt and boots and black hat.

There was no mistaking they were brothers. Years and lifestyles may have kept them apart, but the Elliott genetics were strong. Just the sight of his three brothers had something shifting in Beau's chest. Perhaps he was supposed to be here now, for more than Madelyn.

"Throwing punches took longer than I thought," Nolan growled, closing the distance. "You've been here a whole week."

Beau ignored the comment and glared back at Colt. "You know nothing about me anymore, so don't presume you know what type of man I am."

"Whose fault is that?" Colt shouted. "You didn't let us get to know the man you grew into. We had to watch it on the damn movie screen."

Guilt…such a bitter pill to swallow.

"Why don't we just calm down?" Hayes suggested as he stepped back. "Beau is home now and Dad wouldn't want us going at each other. This is all he ever wanted, us together, working on the ranch."

"You haven't even been to see him," Colt shot at Beau, his dark eyes still judgmental.

"I will."

Colt shook his head in disgust, but Beau didn't owe him an explanation. Beau didn't owe him anything. They may be twins, but the physical appearance was where their similarities ended. They were different men, with different goals. Why should Beau be sorry for the life he'd created for himself?

Nolan reached them then and diverted his attention. "Pepper wanted me to invite you and Madelyn for dinner," he stated in that calm voice of his. "Are you free this evening?"

Beau blew out the stress he'd been feeling and raked a hand along the back of his neck. "Yeah. I'm free. Madelyn's been a little cranky. Scarlett thinks she's cutting teeth, but we should be able to make it."

"Scarlett?" Nolan asked.

"His new nanny," Colt interjected. "She's petite, curvy, stunning. Just Beau's type."

Beau wasn't going to take the bait, not again. Besides, already he knew that Scarlett was so much more than that simple description. She was vibrant and strong and determined…and she'd had his fantasies working overtime.

"You're married," he said instead to his twin. "So my nanny is none of your concern."

"Just stating the facts." Colt held his hands out and took a step back. "I'm happily married with two babies of my own, so don't worry about me trying to lay claim. I'm loyal to my wife."

"Scarlett can come, too, if you want," Nolan added, clearly ignoring his brother's argument. "Pepper won't mind."

Scarlett joining him? Hell no. That would be too familial and definitely not the approach he wanted to take on day one with his temporary help. Not the approach he'd want to take on any day with her, actually.

Not that long ago he would've jumped at the excuse to spend more time with a gorgeous woman, but his hormones were just going to have to take a back seat because he had to face reality. The good times that he was used to were in the past. His good times now consisted of a peaceful night's sleep and a happy baby.

Damn, he was either getting old or finally acting like an adult.

He'd always tried to keep himself grounded over the years, but now that he was home, he realized just how shallow Hollywood had made him. Shallow and jaded. Yet another reason he needed to keep himself and his daughter away from that lifestyle.

"It will just be Madelyn and me," he informed his brother. Then he shifted his attention back to Colt. "Do you want my help around here or not?"

"From the prodigal son?" Colt's jaw clenched, and Beau could see a bruise was already forming there. Colt finally nodded. "I've got most of the guys on the west side of the property mending fences. I'll take your free labor here."

Well, that was something. Maybe there was hope for them after all. Beau decided since they weren't yelling or throwing more punches, now would be as good a time as any to pitch his thoughts out there.

"I want in on the dude ranch, too."

Beau didn't realize he'd wanted that until they all stood here together. But there was no denying his wishes now. Whether he stayed on the ranch or not, he wanted to be part of his father's legacy with his brothers.

Colt's brows shot up, but before he could refuse, Beau went on. "I'm part of this family whether you like it or not and Dad's wish was to see this through. Now, I know you plan to open in just a few months and a good bit of the hard work is done, but that doesn't mean you couldn't use me."

Hayes shrugged. "Wouldn't be a bad idea to have him do some marketing. He'd have some great connections."

Colt's gaze darted to Hayes. "Are you serious?"

"Hayes is right," Nolan added. "I know none of us needs the extra income, but we want Dad's dream to be a success."

Colt took off his hat, raked a hand over his hair and settled the hat back in place. "Well, hell. Whatever. We'll use you until you take off again, because we all know you won't stick."

Beau didn't say a word. What could he say? He knew full well he likely wasn't staying here longterm. He'd returned because of a deathbed promise and to figure out where to take his daughter. Pebblebrook was likely a stepping stone…nothing more. Just like Hayes had said.

Four

Scarlett swiped another stroke of Cherry Cherry Bang Bang on her toes. Beau had taken Madelyn to dinner at his brother's house and told her she didn't need to come.

So she'd finished unpacking—getting all of her panties put away properly. Then she'd caught up on social media, and now she was giving herself an overdue pedicure with her new polish. She wasn't a red type of girl, but she figured with the new move coming and another chapter in her life starting, why not go all in and have some fun? Now that she was admiring it against her dark skin, she actually loved the festive shade.

And that's about as wild as she got. Red polish.

Could she be any more boring?

She never dreamed she'd be in this position at nearly thirty-five years of age: no husband, no children and a changing career.

She was fine without the husband—she could get by on her own, thank you very much. But the lack of children would always be a tender spot and the career change hurt just as much. Not that her career or lack of a family of her own defined her, but there were still dreams she'd had, dreams she'd had to let go of. These days she tried to focus on finding a new goal, but she still scrambled for something obtainable.

Scarlett adored being a nanny, but she simply couldn't continue in that job. Seeing all that she could've had but never would was just too painful.

Ultimately, she knew she had no choice but to walk away from that career. And because she had no family, no ties to this town of Stone River, she'd decided to move away, as well. In a large city like Dallas, surely there would be opportunities she didn't even realize she wanted.

As she stretched her legs out in front of her on the bed, Scarlett admired her toes. If Christmas wasn't the perfect time to paint her toes bright red, she didn't know when would be.

She settled back against her thick, propped pillows and reached for her laptop. In three weeks she'd be starting her new job as assistant director of activities at a nursing home in Dallas. While she was thrilled about the job and the prospect of meeting new people, she had yet to find proper housing. The one condo she'd hoped to rent had fallen through, so now she was back to the drawing board. Her Realtor in the area kept sending listings, but most were too expensive even with her pay raise.

While her toes dried, she scrolled through page after page of listings. She preferred to be closer to the city so she could have some social life, but then the costs just kept going up. She also preferred a small home instead of a condo or apartment, since privacy was important to her. But there was no way her paycheck would stretch enough to make a mortgage payment on a house. The condo she'd wanted to rent had an elderly lady living on the other side, so Scarlett had been comfortable with that setup.

She was switching to a new website when she heard the cabin door open and close. She eased her laptop aside and, after checking that her toes were nice and dry, she padded barefoot toward the living room.

As soon as she stepped through the door, Beau held his finger up to his lips and Scarlett noticed the sleeping baby cradled in his arm…against one very flexed, very taut biceps.

Down, girl.

She'd seen him on-screen plenty of times, but seeing him in person was quite a different image. She didn't know how he managed it, but the infuriating man was even sexier.

Wasn't there some crazy rule that the camera

added ten pounds? Because from her vantage point, she thought maybe he'd bulked up since being on-screen because those arms and shoulders were quite something.

Scarlett clenched her hands, rubbing her fingertips against her palms at the thought of how those shoulders would feel beneath her touch.

She seriously needed to get control of her thoughts and focus. The only person she needed to be gripping, touching or even thinking about was Madelyn.

Scarlett motioned toward her room and whispered, "Let her sleep in here tonight since you didn't sleep last night."

He looked like he wanted to argue, but Scarlett quirked a brow, silently daring him to say one word. He may be the big, bad billionaire, but she wasn't backing down. Part of being a good nanny was to not only look after the child, but also take note of the parent's needs.

When Beau took a step toward her room, Scarlett ushered ahead and pulled the blinds to darken the space over the crib. The moon shone bright and beautiful tonight, but she wanted Madelyn to rest peacefully.

Scarlett took her laptop and tiptoed out of the room while Beau settled Madelyn in her crib. After taking a seat on the leather sofa in the living room, Scarlett pulled up those listings again. The sleeping baby didn't need her right now and she figured Beau had things to do. So, until he told her differently, she wouldn't get in the way.

Moments later, he eased from her room and closed the door behind him.

"I have food for you."

His comment caught her off guard. "Excuse me?"

Beau came around the couch and stood in front of her. That black T-shirt and those well-worn jeans may look casual, but the way they fit him made all her girly parts stand up and take note of just how perfectly built he truly was. Not that she hadn't noticed every other time she'd ever looked at him.

"Pepper, Nolan's wife, insisted I bring you food and she was angry I didn't invite you."

Scarlett smiled, but waved a hand. "No reason to be angry. You didn't need me."

Something flared bright and hot in his eyes, but before she could identify what she'd seen, he asked, "Have you eaten?"

"I had a granola bar, but I'm not really that hungry." She was too concerned with being homeless when she moved to Dallas.

Beau muttered something about needing more meat on her bones before he headed back out the front door. An instant later he came back in with containers and headed toward the open kitchen.

Scarlett set her laptop on the raw-edged coffee table and figured it would be rude if she didn't acknowledge the gesture.

"I could eat a little more," she commented just as her belly let out a low grumble. "What do you have?"

He gestured to the stool opposite the island where he stood. "Have a seat and I'll get you a plate before your stomach wakes my daughter."

As Scarlett eased onto the wooden stool, she couldn't believe her eyes. Hollywood heartthrob Beau Elliott was essentially making her dinner. There wasn't a woman alive who wouldn't want to be in her shoes right now.

Beau pried lids off the plastic storage containers and Scarlett's mouth watered at the sight of mashed potatoes with gravy, green beans, and meatloaf he heaped onto a plate. Mercy sakes, a real home-cooked meal. There was no way she could eat all of that and still button her pants.

"Don't tell me you're one of those women who count every carb," he growled as he spooned a hearty dose of potatoes onto a plate.

"Not every carb, but I can't exactly afford to buy bigger clothes."

He shook his head as he once he filled the plate he placed it in front of her. He pulled open a drawer and grabbed a fork, passing it across, too.

"What would you like to drink? I haven't been the best at keeping food in here for me," he stated as he walked to the fridge. "I have formula, cereal, organic baby juice or water."

Wasn't it adorable that everything in the kitchen was for a five-month-old? But, seriously, what on

earth was the man going to live on? Because someone as broad and strong as Beau needed to keep up
his stamina…er, energy.

*Do not think about his stamina—or his broad
shoulders. Or tracing those tattoos with your tongue.*

"Water is fine, thanks."

She decided the best thing to do was just shovel
the food in. She may regret overeating later, but at
least her mouth would be occupied and she couldn't
speak her lascivious thoughts.

"I'll take Madelyn and make a grocery run tomorrow," she offered as she scooped up another bite of
whipped potatoes.

Beau opened one cabinet after another, clearly
looking for something. "I don't expect you to do the
work of a maid."

"Then who will do it?" she countered before she
thought better of it. But then she opened her mouth
again and charged forward. "Either you have to go
or I have to, unless you want the media to chase
you through aisle seven and see what type of toilet
paper you buy."

Beau stopped his search and turned to face her.
He flattened his palms on the island and leaned in.

Maybe she'd gone too far, but seriously, who
would do the shopping? Surely not his brothers,
who were obviously not taking Beau's homecoming
very well, for reasons that were none of her concern
but still inspired her curiosity. Still, she probably

should've left that last part off, but she'd never had a proper filter.

"Are you always this bold and honest?" he asked.

Oh, he didn't want her complete honesty. Was this a bad time to tell him she'd been holding back?

Scarlett set her fork down and scooted her plate back. Resting her arms on the counter, she cocked her head.

"I believe in honesty at all times, especially in this line of work. But I really am just trying to make things easier for you."

He stared at her another minute and she worried that she had a glob of gravy in the corner of her mouth or something, but he finally shook his head and pushed off the counter.

"You don't have to go," he told her. "I can ask one of my sister-in-laws to pick some things up for me."

As much as she wanted to call him out on his bullheadedness, she opted to see a different side. She may not know the dynamics of his family or the stormy past they'd obviously had, but she recognized a hurt soul when she saw one.

"I'm perfectly capable of grocery shopping," she stated, softening her tone. "I've lived on my own for some time now and besides, you wouldn't be the first client I've shopped for."

Beau folded his arms across his broad chest and leaned back against the opposite counter. "And where do you live?"

Her appetite vanished, pushed out by nerves as she pondered her upcoming move.

"Currently here."

"Obviously." His dry tone left no room for humor. "When you're not taking care of children, where do you call home?"

Between his intense stare and the simple question that set her on edge, Scarlett slid off the bar stool and came to her feet.

"I have no home at the moment," she explained, sliding her hands in the pockets of her jeans. "I'm still looking for a place."

Beau's dark brows drew in, a familiar look she'd seen on-screen, but in person... Wow. That sultry gaze made her stomach do flips and her mouth water. She didn't care if that sounded cliché, there was no other way to describe what happened when he looked at her that way.

"You're only here three weeks," he stated, as if she'd forgotten the countdown.

Scarlett picked up her plate and circled the island. She covered the dish up and put it inside the fridge. She needed to do something to try to ignore the fact that she wasn't only under the same roof as Beau Elliott, she was literally standing within touching distance and he was staring at her as if he could see into her soul.

No, that wasn't accurate at all. He was staring at her as if she stood before him with no clothes.

Maybe she should've kept that island between them.

"I'm moving to Dallas," she explained, trying to stay on topic. "This is my final job with the Nanny Poppins agency."

The harsh reality that this was it for her never got any easier to say. But, hey, if she had to leave, at least she was going out on the highest note of her nanny career. Staying with Hollywood Bad Boy Beau Elliott and taking care of his precious baby girl.

"Why the change?" he asked. "You seem to love your job."

The burn started in her throat and she quickly swallowed the emotions back. This was the way things had to be, so getting upset over it would change absolutely nothing. She might as well enjoy her time here, with the baby and the hunk, and move on to the new chapter in her life.

New year, new start, and all that mumbo jumbo. This was the second time in her life she'd started over on her own. If she did it when she was younger, she could certainly do it now.

"Why don't you get me a grocery list and I'll take Madelyn when she wakes in the morning," she said.

Scarlett started to turn, but a warm, strong hand curled around her bare biceps. She stilled, her entire body going on high alert and responding to the simplest of touches.

But this wasn't a simple touch. This was Beau Elliott, actor, playboy, rancher, father. Could he be more complex?

When he tugged her to turn her around, Scarlett

came face-to-face with a sexy, stubbled jawline, firm mouth, hard eyes.

No, not hard, more like…intense. That was by far the best adjective to describe her boss. There was an intensity that seemed to radiate from him at all times, and that powerful stare, that strong, arousing grip, had her heart pounding.

"Women don't walk away from me."

No, she'd bet not. Most likely he gave them one heavy-lidded stare or a flash of that cocky grin and their panties melted off as they begged him for anything he was willing to give.

"I'm not walking away from you," she defended. "I'm walking away from this conversation."

"That's not fair." He still held on to her arm and took a half step closer until his torso brushed against hers. "I guarantee you know more about me than I know about you."

Scarlett laughed, more out of nerves than humor. "That's not my fault you parade your life in front of the camera. You know all you need in order for me to do my job."

The hold he had on her eased, but he still didn't let go. No, now he started running that thumb along the inside of her elbow.

What the hell?

She'd say the words aloud, but then he might stop and she wanted to take this thrill and save it deep inside her memory. So what if this was all wrong and warning flags were waving in her head?

"You don't look like a nanny," he murmured, studying her face. "Maggie looked like a nanny. You…"

Her entire body heated. With each stroke of that thumb she felt the zings down to her toes.

"What do I look like?" she asked. Why did that come out as a whisper?

"Like trouble."

Scarlett wanted to laugh. Truly she did. Of all the words used to describe her, *trouble* certainly had never been a contender.

This had to stop before she crossed the professional boundary. She'd never had an issue like this before, and by issue she meant a client as potent and as sexy as Beau Elliott. No wonder women flocked to him and wanted to be draped over his arm. If she were shallower and had no ambitions, she'd probably beg to be his next piece of arm candy.

But she wasn't shallow and she most definitely had goals…goals that did not include sleeping with a client.

"Make me that grocery list and text it to me," she told him as she took a step back. "Madelyn and I will head out in the morning."

She didn't wait on him to reply. Scarlett turned and fled to her room. She didn't exactly run, but she didn't walk, either. There was no way he wasn't watching her. She could practically feel that heavy gaze of his on her backside.

No doubt Beau knew just how powerful one of

his long looks were. He'd gotten two big awards for his convincing performances and she couldn't help but wonder just how sincere he was with his affection or if he was just trying to find another bedmate.

Scarlett gently closed the door behind her and leaned against it. Over in the corner Madelyn slept. That little girl was the only reason Scarlett was here. There was no room for tingles or touching or…well, arousal.

There, she'd admitted it. She was so turned on by that featherlight touch of Beau's she didn't know how she'd get any sleep. Surely if she so much as closed her eyes, she'd dream of him doing delicious things to her body. That was the last image she needed on this final nanny assignment.

Scarlett moved away from the door and started changing for bed.

One day down, she told herself. Only twenty more to go.

Five

What the hell had he been thinking touching her like that?

Beau slid his cowboy boot into the stirrup and swung his other leg over the back of Starlight, the newest mare to Pebblebrook.

He'd gotten up and out of that house this morning before seeing Scarlett. A niggle of guilt had hit him when he'd slunk out like he was doing some walk of shame, but damn it. He couldn't see her this morning, especially not all snuggly with Madelyn.

He hated not kissing his daughter good morning, but one day would be all right. Perhaps when he got back to the cabin he'd have a little more control over his hormones and unwelcome desires.

Damn it. He'd been up half the night, restless and aching. Likely Scarlett had been sleeping and not giving him another thought. This was all new territory for him, wanting a woman and not being able to have her.

With a clack of his mouth and a gentle heel to the side, Beau set Starlight off toward the back of the property.

Last night, his thoughts volleyed all around. He couldn't help wondering what Scarlett planned on doing when she left the agency, or why she was even leaving in the first place, but what kept him up all night was wondering what the hell she slept in.

Maybe she had a little pair of pajamas that matched that bright red polish she'd put on her toes. Mercy, that had been sexy as hell. He was a sucker for red.

Beau gripped the reins and guided the beautiful chestnut mare toward Hayes and Alexa's house. Beau hadn't been to the old, original farmhouse nestled in the back of the ranch since coming home. It was time he ventured out there and started making amends with his brothers. So what if he was starting with the one least pissed at him?

When Hector had been diagnosed with the inoperable brain tumor, Beau had known things weren't going to end well for them. Hector had been so much more than an agent. He'd been like a father figure, pulling Beau from the mess he'd gotten himself into when he'd first hit LA. For years they'd been like one unit, and then Beau's foundation was taken away.

But Hector had made Beau promise to go home and work on the relationships with his brothers and father. So, here he was. Having a sexy woman beneath his roof was just added penance. It was like fate was mocking him by parading Scarlett around like some sweet dream that would never become reality.

Which was why he'd been scolding himself all morning.

He couldn't touch her again. First of all, he'd put her in an uncomfortable position. That wasn't professional and he probably owed her an apology…but he wasn't sorry. He wasn't sorry that he'd finally gotten to touch her, to inhale that sweet, floral scent and see the pulse at the base of her neck kick up a notch.

Second of all, he couldn't touch her again because last night he'd been about a half second from jerking that curvy body against his to see exactly how well they'd fit.

He felt his body react to that thought, and forced his mind onto something else. The weather. That was innocuous enough. He looked around. The morning sun was warming up and already burning off the fog over the ranch.

He hoped the ice around Colt's heart would burn off just as easily. Granted, the cold welcome Beau had received was his own fault. Still, Colt acted like he didn't even want to try to forgive. Maybe that was just years of anger and resentment that had all built up and now that Beau was home Colt felt justified to unload.

But Christmas was only a few weeks away, and Beau wondered if he'd even be welcome at the table with the rest of the family. Hopefully by then, the angry words would be out of the way and they could start moving forward to a more positive future.

Beau had a movie premiere just two days before Christmas, but he planned on being gone only two days and returning. There was nothing he wanted more than to have his daughter at the ranch during the holiday and with the rest of the family.

Beau's cell vibrated in his pocket, but he ignored it. Instead, he kept Starlight at a steady pace and let himself relax as they headed to the back of the estate. He'd ridden horses for movie roles, but nothing was like this. No set could compare to being on his own land, without worrying about what direction to look or how to tip his hat at just the right angle for the camera, but not to block his eyes.

Being out here all alone, breathing in the fresh air and hoping to sew up the busted seams of his relationships kept Beau hopeful.

And really, his future depended on how things went over the next few weeks. Apologizing and crawling home with his proverbial tail between his legs wasn't easy. Beau had his pride, damn it, but he also had a family that he missed and loved.

If Christmas came and there was still no further

progress made with Colt, Beau would go. He'd take Madelyn and they would go…somewhere. Hell, he had enough homes to choose from: a mansion in the Hollywood Hills, a cabin in Montana, a villa in France, his private island off the coast of Italy. Or he could just buy his own spread and build a house if that's what he chose. Maybe he'd start his own ranch and show Madelyn the way he was brought up.

But he wanted Pebblebrook.

The cell continued to vibrate. Likely his new agent, worried Beau had officially gone off-grid. Maybe he had. Maybe he wouldn't emerge until the premiere in a few weeks—maybe not even then. He didn't necessarily want to go to the premiere, but this was the most anticipated holiday movie and the buzz around it had been bigger than anything he'd ever seen.

Apparently *Holly Jolly Howards* struck a chord with people. The whole family falling apart and finding their way back together after a Christmas miracle saved one of their lives was said to be the next holiday classic. Move over *White Christmas* and *It's a Wonderful Life*.

Getting his on-screen family back together had been easy. All he'd had to do was act out the words in the script. But in real life, he was on his own.

Beau had only been back in Pebblebrook a short time, but already there was a peacefulness that calmed him at times like this. Just being out in the open on horseback helped to clear his mind of all the chaos of the job, the demands of being a celebrity, and the battle he waged with himself.

These past several months since becoming a parent had changed his entire outlook on life. He wanted the best for Madelyn, and not just the best material things. Beneath the tailor-made suits, the flashy cars and extravagant parties, he was still a simple man from a Texas ranch. He'd always had money, so that wasn't anything overly important to him.

He wanted stability. He knew it was vital in shaping the future of a child. The simplicity of routine may sound ridiculous, but he'd found out that having a schedule made his life and Madelyn's so much easier. She needed to have a life that wasn't rushing from one movie set, photo shoot, television interview or extravagant party to another. That whirlwind lifestyle exhausted him; he couldn't imagine a baby living like that.

Beau may have a nanny now, but that's not how he wanted to live his entire life. He wasn't kidding when he said he wanted to be a hands-on father. He wouldn't be jetting off to various locales just to have someone else raise his daughter.

As Hayes's white farmhouse came into view, guilt reacquainted itself with Beau. His parents had done a remarkable job of providing security and a solid foundation for the four Elliott boys.

Once their mother passed, that foundation was shaken and everyone had to figure out their purpose. Beau had started getting that itch to see if there was something else out there for him. Since money hadn't been an issue, he'd taken a chunk out of his college fund and headed to Hollywood, despite his father's demands to stay.

The cell in Beau's pocket vibrated once again as he pulled his horse up to Hayes's stable. He dismounted and hooked the rein around the post. When he turned toward the house, Alexa stepped out the back door and her son, Mason, came barreling out past her.

Beau smiled, loving how his brother had found this happiness. They'd even decorated the house for the holidays. Sprigs of evergreen seemed to be bursting from the old wagon in the yard, a festive wreath hung on the back door, and red ribbons were tied on the white posts of the back porch.

"Hope you don't mind me stopping by," Beau said as he approached the steps. "I figured I should get to know my new family members a little better."

Alexa crossed her arms and offered a welcoming grin. "Never in my life did I think I'd meet a movie star, let alone have one for a soon-to-be brother-in-law."

Mason stopped right in front of Beau and stared up at him. "Hi."

Beau tipped his hat back and squatted down to the little guy. "Hey, buddy," he greeted. "How old are you?"

Mason held up one finger and smiled. Beau had already been educated on the ages of his nieces and nephews. This was just another reason he wanted Madelyn here. This new generation of Elliotts should be close, because when your life went to hell and got flipped upside down, family was invaluable.

Beau thought of his brother Colt's reaction yesterday. Part of him knew that if Colt didn't care, he wouldn't be acting like a wounded animal right now. The ones you loved most had the ability to cause the most pain.

"Why don't you come on in," Alexa invited. "Mason and I were just about to make some muffins to take to Annabelle this afternoon. She's got her hands full at the B and B, so I offered to help. I'm not a great baker, but I can make muffins."

"I don't want to interrupt."

Alexa raised her brows. "Yet you rode out here without calling or texting?"

She offered a wide smile and waved her hand. "Get in here. Family doesn't interrupt."

Beau could see how Hayes hadn't stood a chance with this one. She was sassy and headstrong...pretty much like the sultry seductress down in his cabin.

Granted, Scarlett didn't have a clue how his stomach knotted up just thinking of her, how he'd been in a tangle of sheets all night because...well, the fantasies wouldn't let him sleep.

Mason lifted his arms toward Beau. Without hesitation, Beau picked up his...well, this would be his nephew. He hadn't been around children until he'd had his own. Oh, there were a few on some sets that he worked with, but they weren't his responsibility or they were a little older and so professional, they didn't act like regular kids.

But this little guy didn't care that Beau had two shiny acting awards back at his Hollywood Hills mansion. He didn't even know who Beau was or why he was here. Mason wanted affection and he was open and trusting and ready to accept the comfort of a stranger.

If only the rest of the family could be as welcoming as a child.

"Hayes actually just ran into town to get more supplies at the store," Alexa stated as she stepped into the house and held the door open for him. "I offered, but he keeps saying he needs to get out more."

Which was a huge accomplishment in itself. Suffering from PTSD had kept Hayes hidden away and everyone shut out for too long. Alexa had pulled him out of the rubble he'd buried himself in. The love of a good woman, Beau reckoned, was clearly invaluable. All of his brothers had found their perfect soul mate and secured a happy future.

There was clearly something in the water on Pebblebrook Ranch. No way in hell was he drinking from the well. The last thing he needed was more commitment or a relationship to worry about. Maybe one day—maybe—but not now.

Beau stepped into the kitchen and stilled. "Wow."

Alexa smiled. "I know. Hayes did an amazing job of renovating this place, though he did take my advice on the kitchen and use some of my Latino heritage as inspiration."

Judging by the bold colors from the blue backsplash to the yellow and orange details in random tiles on the floor, there was no doubt Hayes had made his fiancée feel part of this renovation.

"I haven't been back," he murmured as he held on to Mason and stepped farther into the room. "I'm going to need a tour."

Alexa reached for an apron on the hook by the pantry doors. "I'm going to let Hayes do that," she stated. "I'd say you two need some time alone."

The back door opened and Beau spun around to see his brother step in carrying bags of groceries.

"That place was pure hell," he growled as he set everything on the raw-edge kitchen table. "Remind me never to go in the morning again. Every senior citizen from town was there, all wanting to talk or shake my hand."

Beau knew his brother was grateful for the people who appreciated his service to their country, but Hayes had never been one for accolades.

"That's because they're thankful for your service." Alexa laughed and crossed to Beau. She lifted Mason from his hands. "Your brother wants a tour of the house. Now, go do that and let me work on these muffins so Annabelle doesn't have to do everything for her guests."

Annabelle, Colt's wife and owner of the bed-and-breakfast next door, was not only the mother of nearly two-year-old twin girls, rumor had it she was also a phenomenal chef. Beau had the utmost respect for her because he could barely make a bowl of cereal and care for Madelyn at the same time.

Hayes eyed his brother and Beau slid off his cowboy hat and hooked it on the top of a kitchen chair. "Care to show me what you did to the place?"

"Are we rebuilding the brotherly bond?" Hayes asked.

"Something like that."

Hayes stared another minute before giving a curt nod. "Let's go, then."

Beau followed Hayes out of the kitchen and caught Alexa's warm smile and wink as he left.

They stepped into the living room, and Beau noticed the old carpet had been replaced with wide-plank wood flooring. The fireplace and mantel had been given a facelift. The room glowed with new paint, new furniture.

The fireplace had garland and lights draped across it, as well as three knitted stockings. A festively decorated Christmas tree sat in the front window. Presents were spread all beneath and Beau figured Hayes may have gone a bit overboard with the gifts for Mason.

Everything before him, from the renovations to the holiday decor, was the sign of a new chapter in his brother's life.

Beau wanted to start a new chapter, but he couldn't even find the right book for his life.

"We'll start upstairs," Hayes said over his shoulder. "That way I can grill you without Alexa overhearing."

Beau mounted the steps. "Why do you think I came here instead of Colt's? I'm easing into this rebonding process."

Hayes reached the landing before making the turn to the second story. "Heard you went to Nolan's last night. Does that mean Colt is tomorrow?"

Beau shrugged. "We'll see."

"And Dad?"

Beau stood on the narrow strip with his brother and stared into familiar dark eyes. "I'll get there," he promised.

Hayes seemed as if he wanted to say more, but he turned and continued on upstairs. "Then we can discuss your nanny while I show you what I did with the place."

Great. As if she hadn't been on his mind already. She actually hadn't gotten *off* his mind since she'd showed up at his door looking like she'd just stepped off a calendar for every male fantasy. The fake women in LA didn't even compare to the natural beauty of Scarlett Patterson.

"There's nothing to know about her," Beau stated, hoping that would end the conversation, but knowing better.

"Here's the guest bath." Hayes motioned toward the open doorway, but remained in the hall. "We gutted it and started from scratch. So, Scarlett replaced Maggie. That was quite a change."

"That wasn't a very smooth transition from the bath to the nanny."

Hayes merely shrugged and leaned against the door frame, clearly waiting for an answer.

Returning his attention to the renovated bath, Beau glanced around at the classy white and brushed nickel decor. He was impressed with all the work that went into the restoration, but he couldn't focus. Just hearing Scarlett's name had his body stirring. It had simply been too long since he'd been with a woman, that's all. It wasn't like he had some horny hang-up over his nanny. For pity's sake, he was Beau Elliott. He could have any woman he wanted.

Yet he wanted the one with a killer body, doe-like eyes, a layer of kickass barely covering a heavy dose of vulnerability. The fact that she cared for his daughter above all else and wasn't throwing herself at him was just another piece in the puzzle that made up this mystery of emotions.

His cell buzzed again and this time Beau pulled his phone out, grateful for the interruption so he could stop the interrogation.

The second he glanced at the screen, though, he barely suppressed a groan at the sight of four voice mails and three texts. The texts, all from his new agent, were frantic, if the wording in all caps was any indicator.

"Problem?" Hayes asked.

Beau read the messages, but ignored the voice mails. "The movie I have coming out is getting in the way of my sabbatical."

Hayes crossed his arms and leaned against the wall. "Is that what this is? You're just passing through until something or someone better comes along?"

Beau muttered a curse and raked his hand through his hair. "Hell, that didn't come out right. I just... I have no clue what I'm doing and it's making me grouchy. My agent and publicist have scheduled so many media slots for me to promote this movie, but I've told them I need to cancel. I'll do call-ins, but I'm not going to LA or New York right now to appear on talk shows."

He simply couldn't handle it. First, he wasn't dragging Madelyn to every event because they lasted from early morning until late at night. Second, well, he needed a damn break.

"You're a good dad."

Beau jerked his attention to Hayes, surprised by his brother's statement. "Thanks. My agent, he tried to get me to take Madelyn and basically use her for more publicity. I won't do that. Jennifer tried and I won't have it. I want Madelyn as far away from the limelight as possible."

Hayes nodded, whether in understanding or approval Beau didn't know. Perhaps a little of both.

"Maybe now you can see a little where Dad was coming from."

Hayes muttered the statement before moving

on down the hall like he hadn't just delivered a jab straight to the heart of the entire matter.

Beau respected the hell out of his brothers and his father. Perhaps because they all had chosen one path and been happy with their lives. Beau had thought he'd been happy and on the right path, until he became a father and his ex had decided drugs and wild parties and a future as a star were much more important.

"Show me what else you've done with the house," Beau said, shoving his cell back in his pocket.

"Don't you need to call someone?"

"This is more important."

Hayes offered a half grin, which was saying something for his quiet, reserved brother. "There's hope for you yet. But we're still going to circle back to Scarlett."

Of course they were, because why not? He'd left the house to dodge her for a bit, but now he was forced to discuss her. There was no end in sight with that woman.

Well, in less than three weeks there would be an end.

But he had a feeling she'd haunt his thoughts for some time.

Six

Scarlett handed Madelyn another fruit puff while she sat in her high chair. She wasn't surprised Beau wasn't here when she'd gotten home from the store.

Home. No. Pebblebrook wasn't her home by any means.

Yet she'd gone a tad overboard purchasing Christmas items to decorate the place. But she couldn't pass them by. She only hoped Beau didn't mind.

She busied herself putting together one of her favorite dishes. She'd come here in such a hurry and at the last minute, she had no clue if Beau had food allergies or what he liked.

Madelyn smacked her hands against the high

chair tray and made little noises then squeals. Her little feet kicked and Scarlett smiled.

As much as being with a baby hurt her heart, Scarlett couldn't deny it was something she'd missed. Madelyn was such a sweetheart and so easy to care for. The few times she'd fussed with her swollen gums had passed quickly, thanks to cold teething rings.

Once the casserole was assembled and put into the oven, Scarlett unfastened Madelyn from the high chair. Madelyn let out high-pitched happy squeals and Scarlett's heart completely melted. Babies had their own language, no doubt about it.

"You need a bath," Scarlett crooned. "Yes, you do. You have sticky fingers and crazy hair."

The click of the front door had Scarlett shifting her focus from the baby to the sexy man who filled the doorway. The second he stepped inside, his dark eyes met hers. Even from across this space, she felt that intense stare all through her body. Those eyes were just as potent as his touch.

For a moment, Beau didn't move and she wondered what he was thinking. She really wished he'd say something to ease the invisible charge that crackled between them.

Scarlett finally broke eye contact, needing to get beyond this sexual tension because suddenly she was getting the idea that it wasn't one-sided anymore. And that could be trouble.

Big trouble.

"I just put dinner in the oven," she stated as she held on to Madelyn and circled the island. "I'm about to give Madelyn a bath."

The front door closed, then the lock clicked into place. Beau slid his black hat off his head and hung it on a peg by the door. Finally, his gaze shifted from her and roamed around the open cabin.

"What's all that?" he asked, nodding toward the sacks lining the sofa and dotting the area rug.

Madelyn reached for Scarlett's hair and tugged. "Just some Christmas decorations," she said, pulling her hair from the baby's sticky grasp.

Beau propped his hands on his hips and shook his head. "Give her to me. I'll give her a bath."

"Are you sure? I don't mind at all."

Beau stepped toward her, that long stride closing the distance between them pretty quickly. "I'll do it."

He slid Madelyn from Scarlett's arms and once he had his daughter, he lifted her in the air and a complete transformation came over him. He smiled, he made silly noises and had the craziest baby-talk voice she'd ever heard.

Well, Maggie had been right on this. Beau was completely different with Madelyn. He may be dealing with his own personal battles, but he wasn't letting that get in the way of his relationship with his baby.

When he went into his room and closed the door, Scarlett figured she might as well tidy up the kitchen. She'd put groceries away, then fed Madelyn when he brought her out, and laid her down for a nap. With time on her hands, she knew she should continue the house hunt. Each day that passed took her closer to her move and it was looking more and more like she'd be in a hotel for longer than she'd anticipated.

But she pushed those worries aside for now, eschewing the laptop for the bags of decorations. She got to work taking the holiday items out of the sacks and figuring where to put them. Considering she was watching every penny, she hadn't bought too much, but now that she was looking at everything in this small space, maybe it was a good thing she'd limited her impromptu spree. But there had been sales and, well, she was a savvy woman who couldn't turn down a bargain—or those little rustic cowboy boot ornaments.

Live garland nestled perfectly on the thick wood mantel. Once the two plaid stockings were in place, Scarlett stood back and smiled. This was already starting to look like home. Not for her, but for the little family in the other room.

She tried to take into consideration Beau's tastes, though she didn't know him well. At least she'd kept the decor more toward the masculine side. Though it had been difficult to leave behind the clearance garland with kissing reindeer and red sparkly snowflakes.

For reasons she couldn't explain, there wasn't a tacky Christmas decoration she didn't love.

Before Scarlett could go through the other bags, the oven timer went off.

She'd just set the steaming casserole dish on the stovetop when Beau stepped from his bedroom. He had Madelyn in a red sleeper with little reindeer heads on the feet. The baby looked so cute, but it was the man who drew her eyes like a magnet. Beau looked so sexy, his chest bare and his jeans indecently low on his narrow hips.

She licked her lips, then realized that wasn't the smartest move when his eyes dropped to her mouth. There went that tug on the invisible string pulling them together.

Why did he have to put those tattoos on display? The image of wild horses obviously paid homage to his roots, but she couldn't help it they also encompassed his true spirit of wanting to be wild and free… or maybe he used to be.

Either way, the ink was a distraction she didn't need, yet she desperately wanted to explore. Along with the lean muscles and six-pack abs.

Scarlett cleared her throat. "Dinner is ready."

Beau moved closer, his eyes locked on hers as if he could read her thoughts. "Is that why you're staring at my chest?"

Scarlett blinked and snapped her eyes to meet his. "I was not."

"You're a liar, but I won't report that to your employer." As he handed Madelyn over, he leaned in close and inhaled right by her neck. "Dinner smells good."

That low, gravelly tone sent shivers throughout her body and she nearly gave in to the temptation to close the two-inch gap and touch that gorgeous chest that beckoned her. But before she could move, he turned away and went back into his bedroom. Scarlett just stood there, stock still, wondering what the hell had just happened. What was he doing and why had she almost let herself get caught up in it? Damn it. That behavior was not at all professional.

Done berating herself, she took Madelyn to the portable swing in the living area and fastened her in. Once the music and swing were on, Scarlett went back to the kitchen and started dishing up the casserole. There was no way she was knocking on Beau's door to see if he was coming out to eat. She'd simply make a plate and he could eat when he wanted.

Scarlett had just poured two glasses of sweet tea when Beau stepped from his room. With his wet hair glistening even darker than she'd seen and a fresh T-shirt stretched across his broad shoulders, it was all she could do to force her eyes away.

He eyed the two plates sitting on the island, then he glanced to her. "You don't have to cook for me."

"You're welcome." The snarky reply just came out, so she added, "I had to cook for myself anyway. Hope you like cabbage."

He didn't say a word, but came over and sank onto one of the stools on the bar side of the island.

As he dug in, she watched for a moment and figured he must not hate it. Part of her was relieved, though she didn't know why. What did it matter if he liked her cooking? She wasn't here to impress him with her homey skills.

Scarlett remained on the kitchen side of the island and started eating. The cabbage, bacon and rice casserole was one of her favorites. It was simple, filling, and rather healthy.

"You can have a seat," he told her without looking up from his plate. "I only bite upon request."

Why did she have to shiver at that? Just the idea of his mouth on her heated skin was enough to have her keeping this island between them. She may only "know" Beau from what she'd read online over the years, but she knew enough to realize he was a ladies' man and an endless flirt. And she was just another female in what she was sure was a long line of forgettable ladies.

So the fact that she lit up on the inside and had those giddy nerves dancing in her belly was absolutely ridiculous. She was leaving soon and he'd go on to more women and probably more children.

"I'm fine," she told him. "I'm used to eating standing up anyway."

That wasn't a lie. In fact, when she'd worked in other homes with small children, she'd been happy simply to get her meal hot. Besides, there was no way she'd get close to him. It wasn't so much him she was afraid of but her growing attraction, and she worried if she didn't keep some distance…

Well, she'd keep her distance so they didn't find out.

"I can keep an eye on Madelyn this way," she went on.

Beau glanced over his shoulder to where his daughter continued to swing. Then he jerked around, his fork clattering to the plate.

"What the hell is all that?" he barked.

Scarlett nearly choked on her bite. She took a drink of her sweet tea and cleared her throat. "Christmas decorations. I told you earlier."

His dark eyes shifted straight to her. "I know what you said earlier, but I didn't realize you were taking over the entire cabin. I thought you were putting stuff in your room. Why the hell is it all over my living room?"

"Because it's Christmas."

Why did he keep asking the most ridiculous questions?

"I didn't ask you to do that," he grumbled.

"Well, you didn't ask me to cook for you, either, but you're clearly enjoying it."

He muttered something else before going back to his plate, but she couldn't make it out. And she didn't ask him to repeat it. Instead, they finished eating in awkward silence. Only the sound of the nursery rhyme chiming from the swing broke through the space.

"There's no reason to get cozy here."

His words sliced right through her and she pulled in a deep breath before addressing him.

Scarlett propped her hands on her hips. "Are you talking to me or yourself?"

His dark eyes darted to hers once more. "Both."

"Well, I don't know what's going on in your personal life, but this is Madelyn's first Christmas. She deserves to have a festive place, whether it's temporary or not."

Madelyn started to fuss and Scarlett ignored her plate and went to the baby.

"Eat," Beau stated as he came to stand beside her. "I can give her a bottle and get her ready for bed."

Scarlett unfastened Madelyn and turned off the swing. "I've got her. You worked all day, so finish your dinner."

She didn't wait for his reply or give him an opportunity to argue. She started to make a bottle, but Beau beat her to it.

"Lay her in my room." He kissed Madelyn's head and glanced up to Scarlett. "I'll keep her tonight."

He stood so close, too close. His arm brushed hers, those eyes held her in place. She'd thought they were dark brown, but now she could see almost golden flecks. They were nearly hypnotic, pulling her in as if in a trance she couldn't resist.

But you have to.

The silent warning broke the spell and she cleared her throat.

"You're paying me to watch her," Scarlett told him, pleased when her voice sounded strong. "If you're going to the stables early, then you need your rest."

She should take a step back, but she didn't want to. He smelled too good and looked even better.

"I also said I'm a hands-on dad." He handed over the bottle. "So leave her in my room after she eats."

Scarlett wasn't going to argue with him. She worked for him and this was his child. If he wanted to be woken up during the night, that was his call.

She clutched the bottle in one hand and held the baby in the other as she headed toward his room, leaving him in the kitchen to finish his dinner. The second she stepped into his bedroom, a full-on assault hit her senses. If she thought he smelled good a moment ago, that was nothing compared to the masculine, fresh-from-the-shower scent that filled his space.

The sheets were rumpled and she found herself transfixed by the sight. Just the thought of Beau Elliott in a tangle of dark navy sheets would fuel her nighttime fantasies for years. He was a beautiful man, all sculpted and tan, with just a little roughness about him.

Was it any wonder Hollywood had pulled him into its grasp and cast him in that first film set in the Wild West? He'd been perfect. Captivating and sexy, riding shirtless on his horse. A handsome cowboy straight from a Texas ranch. He didn't just play the part; he was the part.

Scarlett hated to admit how many times she'd watched that exact movie.

She closed her eyes and willed herself to stop the madness of these mind games. Hadn't she vowed not to focus on the man and remain dedicated to the child?

She fed Madelyn and soothed her until she was ready to be laid down. Once she had the baby in her crib, Scarlett turned to leave, but once again her eyes went to that messy king-size bed.

How many days did she have left?

Scarlett closed her eyes and pulled in a deep breath. She would get through this and keep her lustful desires out of the picture.

She tiptoed from the room and gently shut the door behind her. When she came back into the open area, she noted the kitchen had been cleaned up and the dishes were all washed.

She was stunned. Not only at the idea of a celebrity getting dishpan hands, but a billionaire who had employees who likely did everything from his laundry to making his reservations with arm candy dates.

Scarlett nearly laughed at herself. She wasn't going to date Beau; she wasn't even going to be friends with the man. This relationship, if it could be called such, was strictly professional.

She turned from the kitchen and spotted Beau standing in front of the fireplace. With his back to her, Scarlett had a chance to study him…as if she needed another opportunity or reason to ogle. But that shirt stretched so tightly across his shoulders and that denim hugged his backside in all the perfect places.

"I used to want this."

His low words cut through her thoughts and she realized she'd been caught once again staring. He'd known she was back here.

Scarlett took a few cautious steps forward and waited for him to continue. Clearly he was working through some thoughts.

"Christmas as a kid was always a big deal," he went on as he continued to stare at the stockings. "My mom would bake and I remember coming in from the barns and smelling bread or cookies. There was always something in the oven or on the counter."

She continued to listen without interrupting. Whatever he was working through right now had nothing to do with her. But the fact she was getting a glimpse into his personal life only intrigued her more. Scarlett had a feeling not many people saw this side of Beau.

"Mom would pretend that she didn't see Colt and me sneak out a dozen cookies before dinner." He let out a low rumble of laughter. "That poor woman had a time raising four boys and being a loving wife to my dad. She never worried about anything and was so relaxed. I guess she had to be, considering she was in a house full of men."

Beau paused for a moment before he went on. "Christmas was her time to shine. She had every inch of that house covered in garland and lights. I always knew when I married and settled down I wanted my house to be all decked out. I wanted my kids to feel like I did."

Scarlett's heart did a flip and she realized she'd closed the distance and stood so close, close enough to reach out and touch him. She fisted her hands at her sides.

Beau turned to face her. The torment on his face was something she hadn't seen yet. The man standing before her wasn't an actor. Wasn't a billionaire playboy. The man before her was just a guy who felt pain and loss like anyone else.

"I appreciate what you did here for Madelyn," he told her.

Scarlett smiled. "I did it for both of you."

His lips thinned and he glanced down as if to compose himself. "You didn't have to," he said, his gaze coming back up to hers.

"I wanted to."

Before she thought twice, Scarlett reached out, her hand cupping his cheek. She meant to console, to offer support, but his eyes went from sad to hungry in a second.

Scarlett started to pull away, but he covered her hand with his and stepped into her. Her breath caught in her throat at the brush of his torso on hers.

If she thought his stare had been intense before,

it was nothing compared to what she saw now. Raw lust and pure desire.

"Beau."

He dipped his head and she knew exactly what was coming. She also knew she should move away and stop this before they crossed a line neither of them could come back from.

But she couldn't ignore the way her body tingled at his touch, at the passion in his eyes. She desperately wanted him to put that tempting mouth on hers. She didn't care if she was just another woman to him. She wasn't a virgin and she knew exactly what this was and what this wasn't.

It was just a kiss, right?

Beau feathered his lips over hers. The instant jolt of ache and need shot through every part of her body. But then he covered her mouth, coaxing her lips apart as he teased her with his tongue.

He brought their joined hands between their bodies and the back of his hand brushed her breast.

She'd been wrong. So, so wrong.

This was so much more than a kiss.

Seven

Beau had lost his damn mind, yet there was no way he could release Scarlett now. He'd wanted to taste her since she showed up at his doorstep looking like some exotic fantasy come to life.

Alarm bells went off in his head—the ones that usually went off when he was about to make a mistake. He ignored them.

Scarlett's curvy body leaned in, her nipple pebbled against the back of his hand. The way she groaned and melted into him had Beau ready to rip off this barrier of clothing and take exactly what they both wanted.

Beau took his free hand and settled it on the dip in her waist, curling his fingers and pulling her in tighter. She reached up and gripped his biceps as she angled her head just enough to take more of the kiss.

Kiss. What a simple word for a full-body experience.

Beau eased his fingertips beneath the hem of her shirt and nearly groaned when he came in contact with silky skin.

Scarlett tore her lips away and stepped back. Coolness instantly replaced the heat where her body had been. Beau had to force himself to remain still and not reach for her.

She covered her lips with her shaky hand and closed her eyes. "We can't do that."

"We just did." Like hell he'd let her regret this. They were adults with basic needs. "Did you not want me to kiss you?"

She pulled in a breath and squared her shoulders before she pinned him with that stunning stare. "I wanted it. No use in pretending I didn't, considering I nearly climbed up your body."

Beau couldn't help the twitch of a smile. "Then what's the problem?"

"The problem is that I'm your nanny," she volleyed back. "The problem is I won't be another woman in your long line of panty-droppers."

Panty-droppers? Beau laughed. Full from the belly laughter. Well, at least now he knew exactly what she thought.

Scarlett narrowed her dark eyes. "I don't see what's so funny."

"You can't believe the tabloids," he told her. Because he really wanted her to understand, he explained further. "I know everyone thinks I'm a major player, but that perception is fueled by the tabloids. They like to come to their own conclusions and then print assumptions. Just because a woman was on my arm or in my car doesn't mean she was in my bed."

"I won't be in your bed, either."

That smart mouth of hers kept him smiling. "Well, no, because Madelyn is in there. We should use your bed."

Scarlett let out an unladylike growl and turned away. "We are not discussing this."

"What? Sex? Why not?"

Beau started after her, but stopped when she spun back around. "Other than the obvious reason of me being your daughter's nanny, and I really hate clichés, I'll repeat that I won't be another girl in your bed."

Now she was just pissing him off. "You're really hung up on who's in my bed."

"Or maybe I'm just reminding myself not to get caught up in your charm." She propped her hands on her hips and tipped her head. "I realize I may be a challenge and you're not used to people saying no, but we kissed, it's over. Can we move on?"

She had to be kidding. That heat wasn't just one-sided. She'd damn well melted against him. She claimed to always be honest, but she wasn't just lying to him, she was lying to herself.

"Move on?" he asked. "Not likely."

Her dark eyes flared wide. The pulse at the base of her throat continued to beat faster than normal.

Yeah, that's right. He wasn't one to hide the truth, either. There was no way he could just move on now that he'd tasted her and felt that lithe body against his.

"I have no interest in a fling or to be bullied by someone just because they have money and power," she sneered. "I'm going to bed. I'll keep the monitor on in case you need me."

Money and power? What the hell did that have to do with anything? Clearly she had other issues that went well beyond him, this moment and her attraction.

The second Scarlett turned from him, Beau closed the gap between them and curled his arm around her waist, pulling her side against his chest.

"I never make a woman do anything," he corrected. Above all, she had to know he wasn't like that. "We were both very involved in that kiss. If I thought for a second you weren't attracted to me, I never would've touched you, Scarlett."

She shivered beneath him when he murmured her name in her ear. His thumb eased beneath the hem of her shirt and slid over that dip in her waist.

"Tell me who hurt you," he demanded, his tone firm, yet low.

He didn't like the idea of any woman being hurt by a man, but something about Scarlett made him want to protect her, to prevent any more pain in her life.

Scarlett stiffened and turned those dark eyes up to his. There was a weakness looking back at him that he recognized. He'd seen that underlying emotion every single day in the mirror for the past year. Whatever she was battling, she was desperately trying to hide it. Damn it, he knew how difficult it was to keep everything bottled up with no one to talk to, to lean on.

Circumstances as of late had led him to that exact vulnerable point in his life.

Beau hadn't expected a layer of admiration to join the physical attraction, but slowly his take on Scarlett was evolving into something he couldn't quite figure out.

"I won't be here long enough for my personal life to matter to you," she whispered.

"So I can't care about your feelings while you're here?"

Her eyes darted away, looking in the direction of the fireplace. Maybe the holidays were difficult for her, as well. Did she have family? She hadn't mentioned being with them or buying presents or anything that came with sharing Christmas with someone special.

Everything in him screamed that he was walking a fine line with her. He had a sinking feeling she was alone or she'd lost someone. Whatever the reason, the holiday was difficult on her.

Something twitched in his chest, but Beau refused to believe his heart was getting involved here. There was nothing wrong with caring or worrying about someone, even if that person was a virtual stranger. He'd been raised to be compassionate, that's all. Just because he was concerned didn't mean he wanted a relationship.

He stroked his thumb along her bare skin again, reminding himself anything between them should and would stay physical.

Finally, her eyes darted back to his. "I don't think this is a good idea."

The goose bumps beneath his touch told a different story. He feathered another swipe across her waist.

"What part isn't a good idea?"

"The kiss, the touches." She shook her head and stepped away from him. "I'm going to my room. I still need to find housing before my move so I'm not stuck in a hotel forever…and I need some space from you."

"I'll give you space," he vowed. "That still won't make the ache go away. You know ignoring this will only make the pull even stronger."

She took another step away, as if she could escape what was happening here.

"Then we both better hope we can control ourselves until my time here is up."

Well, so far she'd managed to find eight places to rent, all over her budget, she'd done some yoga trying to calm her nerves, and she was now browsing through social media but not really focusing on the posts.

And it was one in the morning.

Scarlett kept telling herself to go to sleep because the baby would need her undivided attention tomorrow and she may even wake during the night.

Honestly, though, there was just no way she could crawl between the sheets when her body was still so revved up. She didn't even have to concentrate to feel his warm breath tickling the sensitive spot just below her ear or the way he kept that firm yet gentle touch just beneath the hem of her shirt. He tempted, teased…left her aching for more of the forbidden.

How dare Beau put her in this position?

Granted, she hadn't exactly resisted that toe-curling kiss. She'd thoroughly enjoyed Beau. She knew he would never force himself on her. No, he'd kissed her because she hadn't been able to hide her desire and that made her just as easy as all the other women he'd charmed. Damn it, she'd told herself to hold it together. It was only three weeks, for pity's sake.

The last thing she needed was a temporary, heated fling with her movie star boss. Other than the obvious working relationship that should keep them apart, she valued herself as more than someone forgettable—because she knew once she was gone, Beau wouldn't remember her.

Scarlett's heart clenched. Her family had forgotten her, as well. When she didn't bow to their wishes or aim to fulfill any political aspirations to round out the powerhouse family, they'd dismissed her as easily as a disloyal employee.

She slid off her bed and stretched until her back popped. She'd like to grab a bottle of water, but if he was out in the living room, then she really should stay put. She hadn't heard him on the monitor, so either he was incredibly stealthy or he hadn't gone to bed yet.

Scarlett eased over to her closed door and slowly turned the knob to peek out. There was a soft glow from the Christmas lights she'd strung on the mantel, but other than that, nothing. She didn't see him anywhere.

Tiptoeing barefoot, she crossed the living area and went into the kitchen. She tried her best to keep quiet as she opened the fridge and pulled out a bottle of water. When she turned, she spotted the bags of Christmas decor she hadn't done anything with yet.

She wasn't sure if she should mention a tree to Beau or just have one appear. Even if it was a small one, everyone needed a little Christmas cheer. She'd seen a tree farm in town earlier and had heard good things about the family-owned business. Maybe she'd check it out tomorrow just to see if they had something that would work in this small space.

Growing up she'd never been allowed to decorate. Her stepfather always had that professionally done. After all, what would their guests say when they showed up for parties and the tree had been thrown together with love by the children who lived there?

Not that Scarlett got along with his kids. They were just as stuffy and uptight as he was. The one time Scarlett tried to have a little fun and slide down the banister from the second floor to the entryway, her step-siblings were all too eager to tattle.

Scarlett crossed the small area and sank down onto the rug. Glancing from one shopping bag to the next, she resisted the urge to look inside. The rattling of bags would definitely make too much noise— besides, she knew exactly what she had left. Little nutcracker ornaments, a few horses, some stars. Nothing really went together, but she'd loved each item she'd seen so she'd dumped them into her cart.

Scarlett uncapped her water and took a sip.

"Can't sleep?"

She nearly choked on her drink, but managed to swallow before setting her bottle on the coffee table beside her.

Beau's footsteps brushed over the hardwood floors as he drew closer. Scarlett didn't turn. She was afraid he'd be in something like boxer briefs and all on display. Not that she was much better. She had on her shorts and a tank, sans bra and panties because that was just how she slept. At least she'd thrown on her short robe, so she was covered. Still, her body tingled all over again at the awareness of him.

She didn't answer him. The fact that she sat on

the floor of the living room at one in the morning was proof enough that she couldn't sleep.

When Beau eased down beside her, Scarlett held her breath. Were they going back for round two? Because she wasn't so sure she could keep resisting him if he didn't back off a little.

Or perhaps that was his plan. To keep wearing her down until he could seduce her. Honestly, it wouldn't take much. One more tingling touch and she feared she'd strip off her own clothes and start begging for more.

There really was only so much a woman could handle.

"I still won't apologize for that kiss."

And here they went. Back at it again.

"But I also won't make this more difficult for you," he quickly added. "I need you and Madelyn needs you."

She exhaled that breath she'd been holding. That was what she'd wanted him to say, yet now that she knew he was easing off, she almost felt cheated.

Good grief. Could she be any more passive-aggressive? She just… Well, she just wanted him, but that wasn't the issue. The issue was, she *shouldn't* want him.

"I'm not sorry we kissed," she admitted. Might as well go for honesty at this point. "But I need this job, so we have to keep this professional."

Now she did risk turning to look at him. He had on running shorts, not boxers, thank God. But then she raised her eyes and saw that he wore shorts and nothing else.

Why could men get away with wearing so little? It simply wasn't fair. It sure as hell wasn't fair, either, that he looked so perfectly...well, perfect.

"You have somewhere to put all of this?" he asked, nodding toward the bags.

Scarlett nodded, pulling her attention from that bare chest to the sacks. "On the tree."

"I don't have a tree."

"I plan on fixing that very soon."

When he continued to stare at her, she didn't look away. Scarlett stretched her legs out in front of her and rested her hands behind her, daring him to say something negative about Christmas or decorations.

"I assume you saw the Christmas tree farm down the road?" he asked.

Scarlett nodded. "I believe Madelyn and I will go back into town tomorrow and check it out. I'll just get something small to put in front of the patio doors."

"Were you going to ask?"

"Like you asked about kissing me?"

Damn it. She hadn't meant to let that slip, but the snark just came out naturally. The last thing she could afford was for him to know she was thinking of him, of that damn kiss that still had her so restless and heated.

"Forget I said that." She shook her head and looked down at her lap. "I'm—"

"Right," he finished. "I didn't ask. That's because

when I see what I want, I just take it. Especially since I saw passion staring back at me."

He didn't need to say he wanted her—she'd gotten that quite clearly. Most likely she appealed to him because she hadn't thrown herself at him or because she was the only woman around, other than his brothers' women.

Beau slid his finger beneath her chin and forced her to look at him. Oh, that simple touch shouldn't affect her so, but it did. She was human, after all.

"What makes you so different?" he muttered beneath his breath, but she heard him.

Scarlett shifted fully to face him. "What?"

Beau shook his head, almost as if he'd been talking to himself. That fingertip beneath her chin slid along her jawline, gentle, featherlight, but she felt the touch in every part of her body. The stillness of the night, the soft glow of the twinkling lights just above Beau's head had her getting wrapped up in this moment. She told herself she'd move away in a second. Really, she would.

Beau didn't utter a word, but his eyes captivated her, held her right in this spot. He feathered his fingertips down the column of her neck and lower to the V of her robe. She pulled in a deep breath and tried not to stare at those tattoos on his chest that slid up and disappeared over his shoulder. If she looked at his body, then she'd want to touch his body.

Scarlett clenched her fists in her lap. The robe

parted slightly, and her nipples puckered in anticipation.

"Beau," she whispered.

His eyes dropped to where his hand traveled and explored, then he glanced back up to her. "I want you to feel."

The raw statement packed a punch and Scarlett wasn't sure what he wanted to happen, but she definitely felt. Just that soft touch had her body tingling and burning up.

He dropped that same hand to the top of her bare thigh and she stilled. Those dark eyes remained locked on hers as he slid his palm up her leg and beneath the hem of her robe.

Scarlett's breath caught in her throat as she glanced down to watch his hand disappear. Beau leaned in closer, his lips grazed her jaw.

"You promised no more kissing," she whispered.

"I'm not kissing you." His warm breath across her skin wasn't helping. "Relax."

Relax? He had to be kidding. Her body was so revved up, there was no relaxing. She trembled and ached and it took every bit of her willpower not to strip her clothes off, lie down on this rug and beg him for every single thing she'd been denying them both.

His fingertips slid beneath her loose sleep shorts. If he was shocked at her lack of panties, he didn't say so and his fingers didn't even hesitate as they continued their journey to the spot where she ached most.

She shifted, easing her legs apart to grant him

access…all while alarms sounded and red flags waved trying in vain to get her attention. All that mattered right now was his touch. Who they were didn't matter. They were beyond that worry and clearly didn't give a damn.

There was only so long a woman could hold out and Beau wasn't an easy man to ignore. Damn it, she'd tried.

Scarlett spread her legs wider, then before she knew it, she was lying back on that rug with Beau propped on his elbow beside her. He slid one finger over her before sliding into her. She shut her eyes and tipped her hips to get more. Did he have to move so agonizingly slow? Didn't he realize she was burning up with need?

"Look at me," he demanded.

He slid another finger into her and Scarlett opened her eyes and caught his intense gaze. The pale glow from the Christmas lights illuminated his face. This wasn't the movie star or the rancher beside her. Right at this moment, Beau Elliott was just a man with basic needs, a man who looked like he wanted to tear off her clothes, a man who was currently priming her body for release.

"Don't hold back." It was half whisper, half command.

Considering she'd had no control over her body up until this point, let alone this moment, holding back wasn't an option.

The way he continued to watch her as he stroked

her was both arousing and intimidating. What did he see when he looked at her? Was he expecting more? Would they carry this back into her room?

Scarlett's thoughts vanished as her body spiraled into release. She couldn't help but shut her eyes and arch further into his touch. He murmured something, perhaps another demand, but she couldn't make out the words.

Wave after wave rushed over her and Scarlett reached up to clutch his thick biceps. He stayed with her until the tremors ceased, and even then, he continued to stroke her with the softest touch.

How could she still be aroused when she'd just been pleasured?

After a moment, Beau eased his hand away and smoothed her shorts and robe back into place. Scarlett risked opening her eyes and found him still staring down at her.

"You're one sexy woman," he told her in that low, sultry tone that seemed to match the mood and the dark of night.

Scarlett reached for the waistband of his shorts, but he covered her hand with his. "No. Go on to bed."

Confused, she drew back and slowly sat up. "You're not—"

Beau shook his head. "I wanted to touch you. I *needed* to touch you. I'm not looking for anything in return."

What? He didn't want more? Did men like that

truly exist? Never would she have guessed Beau to be so giving, so selfless.

Scarlett studied his face and realized he was completely serious.

"Why?" The question slipped through her lips before she could stop herself.

Beau answered her with a crooked grin that had her stomach doing flips. "It's not important. Go on, now. Madelyn will be ready to go early and I need you rested."

When she didn't move, Beau came to his feet and extended his hand. She slid her fingers into his palm and he helped her up, but didn't release her.

"I'll be busy all day," he told her. "I look forward to seeing that Christmas tree when you're done with it."

He let her go, but only to reach up and smooth her hair behind her ears. His eyes held hers a moment before he turned and headed back to his room and silently closed the door.

Scarlett remained in place, her body still humming, and more confused than ever.

Just who was Beau Elliott? Because he wasn't the demanding playboy she'd originally thought. He was kind and passionate, giving and self-sacrificing. There was so much to him that she never would've considered, but she wanted to explore further.

Which would only prove to be a problem in the

long run. Because a man who was noble, passionate and sexy would be damn difficult to leave in a
few weeks.

Eight

Colt eased back onto the patio sofa and wrapped his arm around Annabelle. Lucy and Emily were happily playing on the foam outdoor play yard he'd just put together. With the padded sides and colorful toys in the middle, the two seemed to be perfectly content.

"You're home earlier than usual," Annabelle stated, snuggling into his side. "Not that I'm complaining."

"I knew you would be in between cleaning the rooms and checking new guests in."

She rested her delicate hand on his thigh. Those gold bands on her finger glinted in the late-afternoon sunshine.

"We are actually free for the night," she replied. "The next several days are crazy, but I love it."

He knew she did. Annabelle's goal had always been to have her own B and B where she could cater to guests and showcase her amazing cooking skills.

Colt never could've imagined how much his life would change when this beauty came crashing onto his ranch…literally. She took out the fence in her haste to leave after their first meeting and he had been smitten since.

"You've not talked much about Beau."

Her statement brought him back to the moment and the obvious situation that needed to be discussed…even though he'd rather not.

"What do you want me to say?"

Lucy patted the bright yellow balls dangling on an arch on one side of the play yard. Annabelle shifted in her seat and eased up to look him directly in the eye.

He knew that look…the one of a determined woman.

"I can't imagine how difficult this is for you," she started, then patted his leg. "But think about Beau. Can you imagine how worried he was coming back, not knowing if he'd be accepted or not and having a baby?"

Colt doubted Beau had ever been worried or afraid in his life. He'd likely come home because… Hell, Colt had no idea the real reason. He hadn't actually asked.

"I can see your mind working."

Colt covered Annabelle's hand with his and gave her a slight squeeze. Lucy let out a shriek, but he glanced to see that she was laughing and nothing was actually wrong.

"This is tough," he admitted, hating the vulnerability, but he was always honest with his wife. "Having him back is all I'd ever wanted for so long. I guess that's why I'm so angry now."

"Then maybe you should talk to him about your feelings."

Colt wanted to. He played various forms of the conversation over and over in his mind, but each time he approached Beau, something snapped and the hurt that had been building inside Colt seemed to snap.

"Do you trust me?"

Colt eased forward and kissed Annabelle's forehead. "With everything."

"Then let me take care of this," she told him with that grin of hers that should scare the hell out of him. She was plotting.

Colt wasn't so far gone in his hurt that he wouldn't accept help and he trusted his wife more than anyone.

"I love you," he told her, then glanced to their twin girls. "And this life we've made."

Annabelle settled back against his side and laid her head on his shoulder.

"Let's see if we can make it just a bit better," she murmured.

If anyone could help repair the relationship between him and Beau, he knew it was Annabelle.

Maybe there was hope, because all he'd ever wanted was a close family. That was the ultimate way to honor their father.

Beau glanced over the blueprints of the dude ranch. The cabins, one of which he was using, were in perfect proportion to the river, the creek, the stables. His brothers couldn't have chosen a better spot for the guests to stay.

The mini-prints hung in raw wood frames on the wall of the office in the main stable closest to Colt's house. Beau's eyes traveled from one print to the next. The four original surveys of the land from when their grandfather purchased the ranch were drawn out in quarters. So much was the same, yet so different since he was home last.

A lump of guilt formed in Beau's throat. His brothers had designed this and started construction while he'd been in LA living his own life and dealing with Jennifer and her pregnancy. His father's main goal for his life was to see a dude ranch one day on the Elliott Estate. Now the dream was coming to fruition, but Grant couldn't even enjoy it because he was a prisoner in his own mind. Even if Beau or his brothers managed to bring their father here to see the progress, he'd likely never realize the sight before him, or the impact he had on his boys.

"I was hoping to find you here."

Beau glanced over his shoulder at the female voice. Annabelle, Colt's wife, stood in the doorway with a sweet smile on her face. Her long, red hair fell over both shoulders and she had a little girl on her hip.

"Which one is this?" he asked, smiling toward the toddler.

"This is Emily. Lucy is back at the house for a nap because she didn't sleep well last night."

Emily reached for him and Beau glanced to Annabelle. "May I?"

"Of course."

Beau took the child in his arms, surprised how much different she felt than his own. Granted, there was nearly a year between the two.

"I imagine having twins is quite a chore," he stated. "Do you ever get sleep?"

Annabelle laughed. "Not at first, but they're pretty good now. Lucy is getting another tooth, so she was a bit fussy during the night."

Apparently teeth were a huge deal in disrupting kids' sleep habits.

Emily smacked her hands against his cheeks and giggled. Such a sweet sound. "What brings you to the stables?" he asked Annabelle. "If you're looking for Colt, I haven't seen him today."

Likely because his brother was dodging him, but Beau wouldn't let that deter him. He was here to try to repair relationships and he couldn't give up.

"I'm actually looking for you," Annabelle stated.

"I'd like you to come to dinner this evening. Well, you, Madelyn and Scarlett."

Beau stilled. Dinner with his disgruntled twin brother? Dinner with his baby and his nanny? Why the hell would he want to torture himself?

When he and Colt got a chance to speak about their past, Beau sure as hell didn't want an audience.

There was so much wrong with this dinner invitation. First of all, he wasn't quite ready to settle around a table with his brother and second, he couldn't bring Scarlett. Having her there would make things seem too familial and that would only give her the wrong impression.

Damn it. Beau could still feel her against him, still hear her soft pants and cries of passion. Last night had been a turning point, though what they'd turned to he had no idea. All he knew was they were far beyond nanny and boss—which was the reason she couldn't come to dinner.

"I can tell by your silence you're not thrilled." Annabelle smiled. "Let me rephrase. You will come to dinner and bring your daughter and your nanny."

"Why are you so determined to get me to dinner?" he asked.

Emily reached for her mother and Annabelle took the little girl back. "Because you and Colt need to keep working on this relationship. My husband is agitated and he's keeping his feelings bottled up. The more time you two can spend together, the better off you both will be."

He nodded, not necessarily in agreement, but in acknowledgment of what his sister-in-law had just said.

Beau tipped back his hat. "Why does Scarlett need to join us?"

Annabelle rolled her eyes. "Because it's rude to leave her at the cabin and I imagine she wants some female companionship."

Did she? He'd never asked. Granted, it was difficult to talk about her needs when he'd only been worried about his own—which basically involved touching her, tasting her.

Annabelle's intense stare held him in place and he wrangled in his errant thoughts and let out a deep sigh.

"Does Colt ever win an argument with you?"

A wide smile spread across her face. "Never. We'll see you all at six." Then she turned and headed out of the office.

Beau stared after her until he realized he was still staring at the open doorway. That was one strong-willed woman, which was exactly what Colt needed in his life.

The Elliott men were headstrong, always had been. A trait they'd all inherited, right along with their dark eyes and black hair. Beau figured there would never be a woman who matched him, but that was all right. He had Madelyn and she was more than enough.

He turned back to the blueprints on the opposite

wall and continued to admire what would become of this property. Beau didn't know if his father would ever be able to come see this, but he couldn't help but wonder if he should take a copy of these blueprints to show him. Maybe seeing something that meant so much to him his entire life would trigger some memory.

Beau just wanted to do something, to make it possible for his dad to have some semblance of his past to hopefully trigger the present.

In all honesty, Beau wondered if his dad would even recognize him.

He did know one thing. He couldn't keep putting that visit off. He pulled his cell from his pocket and figured it was time to set up a time to see his father.

Scarlett adjusted the tree once again, but no matter how much she shifted and tilted it, the stubborn thing still leaned…and by leaned she meant appeared as if it was about to fall.

She let out the most unladylike growl, then startled when she heard chuckling behind her.

"Problem?"

Turning toward the doorway, Scarlett tried to keep her heart rate normal at the sight of Beau. First of all, she'd thought she was alone, save for Madelyn. Second, she hadn't seen him since he'd sent her to her room last night, though she'd thought of him all day.

Okay, she'd actually replayed their erotic encounter over and over, which was quite a leap ahead of just

"FAST FIVE" READER SURVEY

Your participation entitles you to:
* ✳ 4 Thank-You Gifts Worth Over $20!

Complete the survey in minutes.

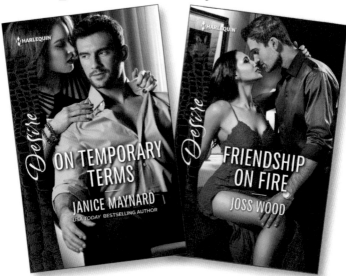

Get **2 FREE** Books

See inside for details.

Dear Reader,

Since you are a lover of our books, your opinions are important to us... and so is your time.

That's why we made sure your **"FAST FIVE" READER SURVEY** can be completed in just a few minutes. Your answers to the five questions will help us remain at the forefront of women's fiction.

And, as a thank-you for participating, we'd like to send you **4 FREE THANK-YOU GIFTS!**

Enjoy your gifts with our appreciation,

Pam Powers

To get your
4 FREE THANK-YOU GIFTS:

✳ Quickly complete the "Fast Five" Reader Survey
and return the insert.

"FAST FIVE" READER SURVEY

1 Do you sometimes read a book a second or third time?   ○ Yes ○ No

2 Do you often choose reading over other forms of entertainment such as television?   ○ Yes ○ No

3 When you were a child, did someone regularly read aloud to you?   ○ Yes ○ No

4 Do you sometimes take a book with you when you travel outside the home?   ○ Yes ○ No

5 In addition to books, do you regularly read newspapers and magazines?   ○ Yes ○ No

YES! I have completed the above Reader Survey. Please send me my 4 FREE GIFTS (gifts worth over $20 retail). I understand that I am under no obligation to buy anything, as explained on the back of this card.

225/326 HDL GM3T

FIRST NAME	LAST NAME

ADDRESS

APT.#	CITY

STATE/PROV.	ZIP/POSTAL CODE

READER SERVICE—Here's how it works:

▲ If offer card is missing write to: Reader Service, P.O. Box 1341, Buffalo, NY 14240-8531 or visit www.ReaderService.com ▲

BUSINESS REPLY MAIL
FIRST-CLASS MAIL   PERMIT NO. 717   BUFFALO, NY

POSTAGE WILL BE PAID BY ADDRESSEE

READER SERVICE
PO BOX 1341
BUFFALO NY 14240-8571

NO POSTAGE
NECESSARY
IF MAILED
IN THE
UNITED STATES

thinking of her hunky roommate. Had Beau thought about what happened? Did the intimacy mean anything to him at all or was this just one-sided?

"The damn tree is crooked," she grumbled.

Beau tilted his head to the side and narrowed his eyes. "Not if I stand like this."

She threw up her hands. "This doesn't happen in the movies. Everything looks perfect and everyone is happy. Christmas is magical and everyone has matching outfits and they go sleigh riding in some gorgeously decorated sled pulled by horses."

Beau laughed as he slid his hat off his head and hung it on the peg by the door. "That's quite a jump from worrying about a tree. Besides, everything is perfect in the movies because decorators are paid a hefty sum to make that happen. Real life isn't staged."

Scarlett turned to stare back at the tree. "It was the only one they had that would fit in this space. I thought I could make it work. Now what am I going to do?"

Beau's boots tapped across the hardwood, then silenced when he hit the rug…the very rug where she'd lain last night and on which she'd been pleasured by this man. She'd tried not to look at it today. Tried and failed.

"Decorate it."

She glanced over her shoulder at his simple, ridiculous answer, but he wasn't looking at her. He only had eyes for his little girl who sat in her swing, mesmerized by the spinning bumblebee above her head.

"How's she been today?"

"Pretty happy." Scarlett stepped around the bags of ornaments and lights she had yet to unpack. "I made some organic food for her so you have little containers in the fridge we can just grab whenever. It's better than buying jars."

Beau jerked his dark eyes to her. "You made her food?"

"I know you want to keep things simple and healthy for her." Now she felt silly with the way he seemed so stunned. "I mean, if you don't want to use it, that's fine, I just—"

"No."

He reached for her arm and Scarlett tried not to let the warmth from his touch thrust her into memories of the night before. But considering they were standing right where they'd made the memory, it was rather difficult not to think of every single detail.

"I'm glad you did that for her," he added, sliding his hand away. "I just didn't expect you to go above and beyond."

Scarlett smiled. "Taking care of children is my passion. There's nothing I wouldn't do for them."

Beau tipped his head. "Yet you're not going to be a nanny anymore when you leave here."

There was no use trying to fake a smile, so she let her face fall. In the short time she would be here, Scarlett really didn't want to spend their days rehashing her past year and the decisions that led to her leaving her most beloved job.

Scarlett stepped around him and turned the swing off. She unfastened Madelyn and lifted her up into her arms. When she spun around, Beau faced her and still wore that same worried, questioning gaze. Not what she wanted to see because he clearly was waiting on her to reply.

Also not what she wanted to see because she didn't want to think about him with those caring feelings. Things were much simpler when she assumed him to be the Playboy Prince of Hollywood.

"Let me get Madelyn settled into her high chair and I'll start dinner." Maybe if she completely dodged the topic, then maybe he wouldn't bring it up again. "Do you like apricots? I found some at the farmer's market earlier and I want to try a new dessert."

Before she could turn toward the kitchen, Beau took a step and came to stand right before her.

"Actually, Annabelle is making dinner tonight," he told her. "She came to the stables earlier and invited me."

"Oh, well. No worries. I'll make everything tomorrow." She brushed her hand along the top of Madelyn's baby curls. "Should I put Madelyn to bed while you're gone or are you taking her?"

Beau cleared his throat and rocked back on his boot heels. "We're all going."

"Okay, then I'll just clean her up and—" Realization hit her. "Wait. We're all going. As in *all* of us?"

Beau nodded and Scarlett's heart started that double-time beat again.

Why on earth would she go to Colt and Annabelle's house? She wasn't part of this family and she wasn't going to be around long enough to form a friendship with anyone at Pebblebrook Ranch. She was trying to cut ties and move on, not create relationships.

"There's really no need," Scarlett stated, shaking her head. "I can make myself something here."

"Annabelle didn't exactly ask," he told her. "Besides, why wouldn't you want to come? The only person Colt will be grouchy with is me."

"It's not that."

Silence nestled between them. She couldn't pinpoint the exact reason she didn't want to go. There wasn't just one; there were countless.

"One meal. That's all this is."

Scarlett stared up at him as she held on to Madelyn. Beau's dark eyes showed nothing. No emotion, no insight into what he may be thinking, but his words were clear. Just dinner. Meaning there was no need to read any more into it.

Was that a blanket statement for what happened between them right here last night? Was he making sure she knew there was nothing else that could happen? Because she was pretty sure she'd already received that message. A message she needed to keep repeating to herself.

"We should discuss last night." As much as she didn't want to, she also didn't want this chunk of tension growing between them, either. "I don't know what you expect of me."

"Expect?" His dark brows drew together.

Why did he have to make this difficult? He had to know what she was talking about.

"Yes," she said through clenched teeth. "You don't think I believe you don't want…something in return."

Beau's eyes darkened as he took a half step closer, his chest brushing her arm that held his daughter. "Did I ask you for anything in return? Did I lay out ground rules?"

Scarlett shook her head and patted Madelyn when the baby let out a fuss. She swayed back and forth in a calming motion.

"Then I expect you to listen to your body," he went on in that low, whisky-smooth tone. "I expect you to take what you want and not deny the pleasure I know you crave. I expect you to come to me when you're ready for more, because we both know it will happen."

Scarlett licked her lips and attempted to keep her breathing steady. He painted an erotic, honest image. She did want him, but would she act on that need?

"You sent me away last night," she reminded him. "If you know what I want, then why did you do that?"

He reached up and slid a fingertip down Scarlett's cheek, over her jaw and around to just beneath her chin. He tipped her head up and leaned in so close his lips nearly met hers.

"Because I want you to ache just as much as I do," he murmured in a way that had her stomach tightening with need. "Because I knew if we had sex last night, you'd blame it on getting caught up in the moment. But now, when you come to me, you'll have had time to think about what you want. There will be no excuses, no regrets."

Her entire body shivered. "You're so sure I'll come to you. What if I don't?"

Beau's eyes locked onto hers and he smiled. "If you weren't holding my daughter right now, I'd have you begging for me in a matter of seconds. Don't try to lie to me or yourself. You will come to me."

"And if I don't?"

She fully expected him to say he'd eventually come to her, but Beau eased back and pulled Madelyn from her arms. He flashed that high-voltage smile and winked. That man had the audacity to wink and just walk away.

That arrogant bastard. He thought he could just turn her on, give her a satisfying sample, then rev her up all over again and she'd just…what? Jump into his bed and beg him to do all the naughty things she'd imagined?

Scarlett blew out a sigh. That's exactly what she wanted to do and he knew it. So now what? They'd go to this family dinner and come back to the cabin, put Madelyn down and…

Yeah. It was the rest of that sentence that had nerves spiraling through her.

Beau Elliott was a potent man and she had a feeling she'd barely scratched the surface.

Nine

Beau was having a difficult time focusing on the dinner set before him. Between his brother's glare at the opposite end of the table, the noise from the three kids, and Scarlett sitting right across from him, Beau wondered how much longer he'd have to stay at Colt's.

He'd left Scarlett with something to think about back at the cabin, but he hadn't counted on getting himself worked up and on edge. That flare of desire in her eyes had given him pause for a moment, but he had to be smart. Wanting a woman wasn't a new experience, but wanting a woman so unattainable was.

The temporary factor of her presence didn't bother him. After all, he wasn't looking for anything long-term. He actually hadn't been looking for anything at all…but then she showed up on his doorstep.

What bothered him was how fragile she seemed beneath her steely surface. He should leave her alone. He should, but he couldn't.

Scarlett wasn't playing hard to get or playing any other games to get his attention. No, she was guarded and cautious—traits he needed to wrap his mind around before he got swept up into another round of lust.

"Scarlett, what are you going to be doing in Dallas?"

Annabelle's question broke into Beau's thoughts. He glanced across the table as Scarlett set her fork down on the edge of her plate.

"I'll be an assistant director of recreational activities at a senior center."

She delivered the answer with a smile, one that some may find convincing. Even if Beau hadn't been an actor, he knew Scarlett enough to know the gesture was fake.

"I'm sad to leave Stone River," she went on. "But Dallas holds many opportunities, which is what I'm looking for. I'm excited. More excited as my time to leave gets closer."

"What made you decide on Dallas? Do you have family there?"

Beau was surprised Colt chimed in with his questions. But considering Beau was curious about more

of her life, he turned his focus to her as well, eager
to hear her answers.

Her eyes darted across the table to him, that forced
smile frozen in place. "I have no family. That's one
of the reasons being a nanny was so great for me.
But circumstances have changed my plans and I'm
looking for a fresh start."

Colt leaned back in his seat and smiled. "Well,
good for you. I wondered if my brother would con-
vince you to stick with him."

Beau clenched his teeth. Was Colt seriously going
to get into this now? Did every conversation have to
turn into an argument or a jab?

"There's no convincing," Scarlett said with a
slight laugh. "I've already committed to the new job.
Housing has turned into a bit of a chore, though. I
didn't realize how expensive city living was."

"Small towns do have perks." Annabelle came
to her feet and went to one of the three high chairs
they'd set up. She lifted one of her twins—he still
couldn't tell the difference—and wiped the child's
hands. "Miss Emily is messy and I need to clean her
up and get her changed. I'll be right back."

Scarlett took a drink of her tea and then scooted
her chair back. "I can start taking these dishes to the
kitchen. Dinner was amazing."

"Sit down." Colt motioned to her. "Annabelle
wanted to make a good impression so she made everything herself, but our cook will clean up."

Scarlett didn't sit, but she went to Madelyn who

played in her high chair, patting the top of the tray, then swiping her hands in the water puddles she'd made by shaking her bottle.

"Let me get her," Beau said as he rose and circled the antique farm-style table to extract her from the high chair. "I haven't seen her much today and when we get back she'll need to go to bed."

Which would leave them alone again. Night after night he struggled. Last night had barely taken the edge off. No, that was a lie. Last night only made him want her even more. She'd come to him tonight, that much he was sure of.

"Never thought I'd see you back at the ranch," Colt stated. "Let alone with a child."

Beau patted Madelyn's back as she sucked on her little fist. "I knew I'd come back sometime, but I never had intentions of having children."

When Lucy started fussing, Colt immediately jumped to get her.

"You plan on settling down anytime soon?" he asked as he picked up his daughter. "Maybe have more kids?"

Beau wasn't sure what his next move was, let alone if there was a woman somewhere in his future. "I have no idea," he answered honestly. "Believe it or not, I did love growing up here and having a large family. I'm not opposed to having more kids one day. Being a parent changes you somehow."

Scarlett cleared her throat and turned away. "Excuse me."

She fled the room and Beau glanced over his shoulder to see her heading toward the front of the house. What was wrong with her? Was it something he'd said? Was she that uncomfortable being at this family dinner?

She didn't owe him any explanations, but that wouldn't stop him from finding out what he could do to make her stay here a little easier. The pain that she kept bottled up gnawed at his gut in a way he couldn't explain, because he'd never experienced such emotions before.

"She okay?" Colt asked.

Beau stared at the empty doorway another minute before turning to his twin and lying to his face. "She's fine. We can head on out if you'd rather. I know Annabelle probably forced your hand into this dinner."

Lucy plucked at one of the buttons on Colt's shirt. "She didn't, actually. I wanted you here and she offered to cook."

Shocked, Beau shifted Madelyn in his arms and swayed slowly back and forth as she rubbed her eyes. "So she jumped at the chance when she saw an opening?"

Colt shrugged. "Something like that. Listen, I don't want—"

"Sorry about that." Scarlett whisked back into the room and Beau didn't miss the way her eyes were red-rimmed. "Let me take Madelyn back home and put her to bed. You two can talk and maybe Colt can bring you back to the cabin later."

"I'll come with you," he offered.

She eased a very tired baby from his arms and shook her head. "I'll be fine," Scarlett said, then turned to Colt. "Please tell Annabelle everything was wonderful."

"I will, though I'm sure she'll have you over again before you leave town," Colt assured her. "I'll make sure Beau has a ride back."

Scarlett nodded and then turned to go, catching Beau's eyes before she did so. Her sad smile and that mist in her eyes undid him. She took Madelyn and left, leaving Beau torn over whether he should stay or go.

"You're really just going to let her go?" Colt asked. "She's clearly upset."

Shoving his hands in his pockets, Beau weighed his options. "She wants to be alone. I can talk to her once I'm back and Madelyn is asleep. Besides, you and I need to talk, don't we?"

Staring at his brother had Colt really taking in the moment. He loved Beau—that was never in question. He loved him in a completely different way than Hayes or Nolan. Not more, just different. Perhaps because of the special bond from twins; he wasn't sure.

Colt knew no matter how much anger and resentment tried to push them apart, their connection could never be completely severed.

"I'm surprised you don't have plans set in place to leave the ranch," Colt stated after a moment.

Or if Beau did, Colt didn't know. And he wanted to…no, he needed to know. He had to steel his heart if his brother was just going to hightail it out of town again and not be heard from for years.

"I came back for Madelyn," Beau replied.

"You came back for you," Colt tossed back, unable to stop himself. "You may have had a change of heart from whatever you were doing in LA, but you needed to be here because something or someone has made you face us again. You didn't come back because you actually wanted to."

Beau stared at him for a minute. Silence settled heavy between them and Colt waited for his brother to deny the accusation. He didn't.

"I've wanted you home for so long." Colt softened his tone. He didn't want to be a complete prick, but he also had to be honest. "When you left, I was upset, but I understood needing to do your own thing. But then you didn't come back and…I resented you. I felt betrayed."

Beau muttered a curse and glanced down to his still-shiny boots before looking back to Colt. "I wanted to see just how far I could get," he admitted. "I knew I was good at acting. So once I did that commercial, then my agent landed that first movie, things exploded. I admit I got wrapped up in my new lifestyle. But I never forgot where I came from. Not once. It just wasn't me anymore."

Colt gritted his teeth and forced the lump of emotions down. "And now? Is this ranch life still not you?"

Beau's lips thinned as he hooked his thumbs through his belt loops. "I want a simpler life for my daughter. I don't want her growing up around pretentious people and worrying if she fits in and all the hustle and bustle. Becoming a parent changed everything I thought about life."

On that, Colt could agree one hundred percent. "Being a father does change you."

But Beau still hadn't answered the question completely.

Before Colt could dig in deeper, Annabelle came back into the room without Emily. "Well, Little Miss was happy lying in her crib in her diaper, so I left her there chatting with her stuffed elephant."

His wife stopped her chatter as she came to stand next to Colt. "What's going on?" she asked as she slid Emily from Colt's arms.

"Just talking with my brother," Colt stated.

"I'm glad to hear it." She rocked Emily back and forth and patted her back. "Where is Scarlett?"

"She took Madelyn back to the cabin for bed," Beau told her. "She wanted me to tell you thanks for everything."

Annabelle shot a glance to her husband. "And did she leave because you guys were bickering or to give you space to actually talk?"

"She really was putting Madelyn to bed," Beau added. "I'm sure she wanted to give us space, too."

"And how has the talking gone?" Annabelle asked, her gaze darting between them. "I lost my sister in a car accident not long ago. We had our differences, we said things we thought we meant at the time, but I'd give anything to have her back. I just don't want you guys to have regrets."

Colt's heart clenched as Annabelle's eyes misted. When he stepped toward her, she eased back and shook her head. Such a strong woman, his Annabelle. He admired her strength and her determination to repair this relationship between brothers.

"You're getting another chance, so work on it," she added. "It's Christmas, guys. Just start a new chapter. Isn't that what your parents would've wanted?"

Beau stepped forward and wrapped an arm around her shoulders. "They would've," Beau agreed before releasing her.

Annabelle sniffed and swiped a hand beneath her eye.

"Babe, don't cry." Colt placed his hand on her shoulder and looked to his twin. "We're making progress. It's slow, but it's coming. Right, Beau?"

He nodded. "We're better than we were, but we're working on years of animosity, so it might take a bit."

Something settled deep within Colt—something akin to hope. For the first time in, well, years, Colt had a hope for the future with his brother.

Did Beau ultimately want that? Colt truly believed

fatherhood had changed him, but they'd have to see because words were easy…it was the actions that were difficult to execute.

"I'll let you guys finish your chat," Annabelle said with a soft smile and left the room.

Colt nodded toward the hallway and Beau followed him to the living room. They truly had taken a giant leap in their relationship.

Once they were in the spacious room with a high-beamed ceiling and a stone fireplace that stretched up to those vaulted beams, Beau took a seat on the dark leather sofa.

They had a full, tall Christmas tree in this room, as well. He couldn't help but laugh. As beautiful as the perfectly decorated tree was, he suddenly found himself longing for the tiny cabin with the crooked, naked tree.

If he were honest with himself, he longed more for the woman in the cabin who was determined to give his daughter a nice first Christmas.

How could he not feel a pull toward Scarlett? Sexual, yes, but there was more. He couldn't put his finger on it…or maybe he didn't want to. Either way, Scarlett was more than Madelyn's nanny.

"Are you planning on leaving Hollywood?" Colt asked as he stood next to the fireplace.

Beau eyed the four stockings and shrugged. "No idea, honestly. I know I don't want that lifestyle for Madelyn. There's too much in my world there that could harm her. I couldn't even take her to a park without the paparazzi attacking us. I just want a normal life for her."

"You gave up the normal life when you chose to pursue acting," Colt sneered. "You had a life here, on the ranch."

Beau shook his head and rested his elbows on his knees. "I'm not rehashing the past or defending myself again. I'm moving on. I won't stay at Pebblebrook, though. There's clearly no room and I'm still not sure what my place is."

"What the hell does that mean?" Colt demanded. "Your place is as an Elliott. You're still a rancher whether you want to be or not. It's in our roots."

Yes, it was. Being back here had been like a balm on his tattered heart and soul. But even with coming home and diving right back into the life he'd dodged for years, something was still missing. His world still seemed as if there was a void, a huge hole he'd never fully be able to close.

Perhaps it was Hector's death. Losing his best friend, his father figure, his agent, was hell. But Beau wondered if being home and not seeing his actual father riding the perimeters or herding cattle was the main reason he felt so empty.

"I'm just trying to figure things out," Beau admitted. "I have a movie premiere a few days before Christmas. I'll have to attend that, and then I'd like to be here for the holidays. I'll go after that."

"And when will you fit a visit to Dad in there?" Colt propped his hands on his hips.

"I'm hoping to go see him tomorrow."

That shut Colt up. Beau knew his brother hadn't expected that comeback and Beau would be lying if he didn't admit he was scared as hell to see his dad. He didn't know how he would feel if he walked into the room and Grant Elliott had no clue who he was.

Ironic, really. He was an award-winning movie star, but the one person in the world he wanted to recognize him was his own father.

"Do you want me to come with you?"

Colt's question shocked him. Beau never expected his twin to offer. Maybe this was the olive branch that Beau wondered if he'd ever see.

He swallowed the lump of emotions clogging his throat and nodded. "Yeah, sure."

Colt gave a curt nod, as well. They may not be hugging it out and proclaiming their brotherly love, but this was a huge step in what Beau hoped was just the first phase in repairing their relationship. Because this process wouldn't be quick and it wouldn't be easy. But it was a start.

Ten

Scarlett continued to stare at the tree mocking her in the corner. The one in Colt and Annabelle's house had looked just like the perfect ones she'd described to Beau. There had even been ornaments on the tree of twin babies with a gold ribbon across that said "Babies' First Christmas."

Scarlett hadn't been able to handle another moment. As much as she wanted to be the woman for Beau, she also knew she could never fully be the woman he wanted...not if he wanted more children and a family.

And this little cabin may not be her home, but Scarlett was determined to give Beau and Madelyn a nice Christmas. Too bad she felt she was failing miserably.

Madelyn had taken a bottle and gone right to sleep, leaving Scarlett alone with her thoughts... thoughts that drifted toward the man who would walk through that door any minute.

So she'd opted to try to decorate this tree. Once the lights went on and she plugged them in, she decided to stop. Maybe this was the best this poor thing would look. The crooked trunk didn't look so bad on the tree lot, but now that it was in the small cabin the imperfection was quite noticeable.

Maybe if she turned it slightly so the leaning part faced the patio doors?

Scarlett groaned. Perhaps she should bake some cookies instead. That would help liven up her holiday spirit, plus the house would smell better than any potpourri or candle she could've bought.

But it was late, so she decided to postpone that until tomorrow. Now she headed to her room to change her clothes, figuring on making some tea with honey to help her relax. She really should make it quickly and get back to her room before Beau came home.

Beau...

He'd tempted her in ways that she'd never been tempted before. Never had a man had her so torn up and achy and...damn it, confused.

She shouldn't want him. There was no good ending to this entire ordeal. They clearly led different lives and he was so used to getting what he wanted, yet another reason why they couldn't work. If she stayed and tried at a relationship, even if he was ready for that, she couldn't ultimately give him what he wanted.

But there were so many turn-ons—so, so many.

Scarlett pulled on a tank and a pair of cotton shorts as she mentally argued with herself. She could either continue to dodge the pull toward Beau or she could just give in to this promised fling. After all, she was leaving in a few weeks. She could have the fling and then move, start her new life and not look back.

He'd already pleasured her, so she knew what awaited her if she surrendered to him. And she knew it would be even better when they actually made love, when his body was taking her to those heights instead of just his hand.

Just thinking about that orgasm caused her cheeks to flush. Yes, that was an even bigger reason to want to agree to everything he'd been ready to give. If that had been part of his master plan the entire time, well then, he'd won this battle.

Fanning her heated cheeks, Scarlett opened her bedroom door…and froze. Beau stood just on the other side, his raised fist poised to knock.

She gripped the doorknob in one hand and tried to catch her breath. Between the surprise of seeing him here and the intense look in his eyes, Scarlett couldn't find a reason to ignore her needs any longer.

Not that she could ignore them even if she wanted to. Not with this gorgeous, sexy, intense man looking at her like he was.

She did the only thing she could do at that moment. She took a step toward him and closed the gap between them.

She kept her eyes locked onto his as she framed his face with her hands. That dark stubble along his jaw tickled her palms, the simple touch sending waves of arousal and anticipation through her, fanning the flames her fantasies had ignited.

"Scarlett—"

She slid her thumb along his bottom lip, cutting off his words. "Do you still want me?"

She had to take charge. She had to know the power belonged to her or he wouldn't just win the battle between them…he'd win the war.

Beau's tongue darted out and slid across her skin as he gripped her hips and pulled her to him, aligning their bodies. There was no mistake how much he wanted her, no mistake in what was about to happen.

She needed this distraction, needed to forget how much she'd hurt earlier seeing all those babies and the happy family. Maybe she shouldn't use him for her need to escape, but she'd wanted him all along and why shouldn't she take what she wanted?

"Why now?" he asked, studying her face. "What changed?"

Scarlett's heart thumped against her chest as she

swallowed and went for total honesty…well, as much as she was willing to share about her pain.

"Sometimes I want to forget," she murmured. "Make me forget, Beau."

The muscle clenched in his jaw and for a moment she wondered if he'd turn her down and leave this room. But then he covered her mouth with his and walked her backward until her back came in contact with the post of the bed.

His denim rubbed her bare thighs, only adding to the build of the anticipation. As much as she loved how he looked in his cowboy wardrobe, she desperately wanted to see him wearing nothing but her.

Beau's hands were instantly all over her, stripping her of her shorts, then her tank. He only broke the kiss long enough to peel away the unwanted material and then he wrapped her back in his strong arms and made love to her mouth.

That was the only way to describe his kisses. He didn't just meet her lips with his; he caressed them, stroked them, laved them, plundered them. And she felt every one of those touches not only on her mouth but in the very core of her femininity.

Needing to touch him the same way, Scarlett reached between them for the hem of his T-shirt. She'd lifted it slightly when his hands covered hers and he eased back.

"In a hurry?" he asked.

She nodded. "I'm the only one ready for this."

"Baby, I've been ready since you walked in my door."

She shivered at his husky tone and glanced down to their joined hands. Her dark skin beneath his rough, tanned hands had her wondering why this looked so…right. Was it just because she hadn't been with someone in so long? Was it because this was *the* Beau Elliott?

She didn't think so, but now wasn't the time to get into why she had these unexplainable stirrings at just the sight of them coming together.

"Someone is thinking too hard. Maybe this will keep your thoughts at bay."

Beau stepped back and pulled off his shirt, tossing it aside. He was playing dirty and he damn well knew it.

As if to drive the point home, he quirked his dark brows as a menacing, sexy smile spread across his face.

"What did you want when you came to my room?" she asked, surprised she even had the wherewithal to speak.

He went to the snap of his pants and shoved them off as he continued to stare at her. He stood before her in only his black boxer briefs and she couldn't keep her eyes from roaming every inch of muscle and sinew on display before her. His body was pure perfection. The sprinkling of dark chest hair and the dark tattoos over his side, pec and shoulder were so sexy. Who knew she was a tattoo girl?

"I wanted to talk," he replied.

"That look in your eye doesn't look like you wanted to talk."

His lips thinned. "Maybe I needed to forget, too."

She crossed her arms and glanced down, suddenly feeling too vulnerable standing before him completely naked as he let a crack open so she could glimpse into his soul.

Beau reached out, unhooking her arms. "Don't hide from me. I've been waiting to see you."

Scarlett swallowed and looked up at him. "You saw me last night."

"Not enough."

His fingertips grazed down the slope of her breasts and around to her sides. She shivered when his hands slid down the dip in her waist, then over the flare of her hips.

"Not nearly enough."

He lifted her by her waist and wrapped his arms around her. Scarlett wrapped her legs around his waist as he carried her to the bed. She slid her mouth along his as she tipped back, then found herself pressed firmly into the thick comforter, Beau's weight on her. She welcomed the heaviness of this man.

The frantic way his hands and mouth roamed over her made her wonder if he was chasing away some demon in his own mind.

Maybe for tonight, they were just using each

other. But right now she didn't care. She wanted him. She needed him. Right now.

When Beau sat up, Scarlett instinctively reached for him to pull him back to her.

"I need to get protection," he told her as he grasped his jeans.

Scarlett hadn't even thought of that. Of course pregnancy wasn't an issue for her, but she didn't know his history and he didn't know hers. Safety had to override hormones right now. She was just glad one of them was thinking straight.

She watched as he removed his boxer briefs and sheathed himself, relishing the sight of his arousal. Nothing could make her turn away or deny this need that burned through her. Well…if Madelyn started crying, but other than that, nothing.

Beau eased his knee down onto the bed next to her thigh. Scarlett rose up to her elbows, her heart beating so fast as desire curled all through her.

He trailed his fingertips up her thigh, teasing her as he went right past the spot she ached most, and on up her abdomen.

"You're one sexy woman," he growled. "It was all I could do to hold back last night."

Which only made him even more remarkable. He wasn't demanding and selfish. Even now, he was taking his time and touching, kissing, enjoying… all while driving her out of her mind.

Those fingertips circled her nipples and Scarlett nearly came off the bed.

"Beau."

"Right here," he murmured as he leaned down and captured her lips.

She opened to him and shifted her legs restlessly. Beau settled between her thighs and she lifted her knees to accommodate him. He hooked one hand behind her thigh and lifted her leg at the same time he joined their bodies.

Scarlett cried out against his mouth as she tilted her hips to meet his. He seemed to move so slow in comparison to the frantic need she felt. The man was maddeningly arousing.

She clutched at his shoulders and arched against him, pulling her mouth from his as she tipped her head back. Beau's lips traveled a path down her neck to her breast and Scarlett wrapped her legs around his waist, locking her ankles behind his back.

Beau never once removed his lips from her skin. He moved all over her, around her, in her, and in minutes that familiar coiling sensation built up within her and Scarlett bit her lip to keep from crying out again.

But Beau gripped her backside, his large powerful hand pulling her to him as he quickened the pace and Scarlett couldn't stop the release from taking over, nor could she stop the cry.

Beau's body tightened against hers as he surged inside her, taking his own pleasure. After a moment, that grip loosened and he eased down onto the bed, shifting his weight so he wasn't completely on top of her.

When the pulsing stopped and her heartbeat slowed, and she was able to think once again, Scarlett realized she was in new territory. She wasn't sure what she was supposed to say or do here. Anyone she'd ever slept with had been someone she was committed to. What did she do now, naked, sated and plastered against a man who was nothing more—could be nothing more—than a fling?

"Someone is thinking too hard again," he said, trailing his finger over her stomach and up the valley between her breasts. "Maybe I didn't do my job well enough."

Scarlett laughed. "You more than did your job. I'm just confused what to do now."

Beau sat up and rested his head in his hand as he stared down at her. The entire moment seemed so intimate, more than the act of sex itself.

"This doesn't have to be anything more than what it was," he told her. "You needed to escape something and so did I. Besides, this was bound to happen."

His words seemed so straightforward and matter-of-fact. They were all true, but she wished he'd…

What? What did she wish? That they'd start a relationship and see where things went? She knew full well where they'd go. She'd be in Dallas and he'd be back in LA. There was nothing for them other than a brief physical connection.

Scarlett shifted from the bed and came to her feet.

Being completely naked now made her feel too vulnerable, too exposed emotionally.

She started putting her sleep clothes back on, trying to ignore the confident cowboy stretched out on her bed.

"Care to tell me what had you running from Colt's house?"

Scarlett pushed her hair away from her face and turned to face him. "I told you. Madelyn was tired and I was letting you guys talk."

He lifted one dark brow and stared, silently calling her out on her lie.

"Could you cover up?" she asked. "I can't concentrate with you on display like that."

Beau laughed and slowly came to his feet...which maybe was worse because now he was closing in on her with that naughty grin. "I like the idea of you not concentrating."

Scarlett put her hands up and shook her head. "Don't touch me. We're done for the night."

He nodded. "Fine, but I still want to know what had you scared or upset."

From his soft tone, she knew he truly meant every word. He didn't care that they weren't diving back in for round two and he genuinely wanted to know what had bothered her.

Scarlett didn't want to get into her emotional issues. Dredging them all up wouldn't change anything, and the last thing she wanted was pity from

Beau. Besides, he'd said he was dealing with his own issues.

"I think it's best if we don't get too personal," she told him and nearly laughed. This was Beau Elliott and women all around the world would give anything to trade places with Scarlett right now.

"We're already personal," he countered, reaching for her. When she tried to back away, he cupped her elbow. "You're taking care of my daughter, living with me and we just had sex. Not to mention my sisters-in-law have all taken to you. We're temporarily bonded, so stop trying to push me away. I can listen and be a friend right now."

Scarlett raked her eyes over him. "With no clothes on?"

He cursed beneath his breath as he spun around and grabbed those black boxer briefs. As if putting on that hip-hugging underwear helped.

The second he turned his focus back to her, she crossed her arms and decided to give the interrogation right back at him.

"Do you want to tell me what's got you so torn up here?" she asked. "Other than your brothers?"

He stared at her for a moment before he shrugged. "I'm not sure what future I have to offer my daughter because I have no clue what I want to do. I'm mending relationships with my brothers, hopefully my father, and figuring out if I even want to go back to LA."

Scarlett couldn't believe he'd said anything, let alone all of that.

"My life is a mess," he went on. "My former agent was more like a father figure and best friend. He recently passed away."

Scarlett put her hand over her heart. "Oh, Beau, I'm sorry."

"Thank you. It's been difficult without him, but each day is a little easier than the last. But the next step is so unclear." He pursed his lips for a moment before continuing. "I have a feeling someone with her new life laid out before her isn't so worried about the future."

"Not when I'm constantly haunted by my past," she murmured.

She rubbed her arms, hating how he was somehow managing to break down her walls. He'd easily opened and didn't seem to care that she saw his vulnerability. Could she do the same?

"I could guess and I bet I'd be right."

She shook her head. "You don't know me."

Beau stepped into her and reached up, smoothing her hair from her face. "You love Christmas and more decorations than anyone needs. You chose the most hideous tree I've ever seen, yet you're determined to make this a good holiday. You're passionate in bed and let yourself lose all control, which is the sexiest thing I've ever seen, by the way."

She stared at him, listening as he dissected her from the nuggets of information he'd gathered over

the past few days. Beau was much more percep-
tive than she gave him credit for. No selfish man
would've taken every moment into consideration and
parsed each portion of their time together to understand her better.

"I also know that my daughter and I are lucky
you're here," he went on, inching even closer until
she had to tip her head to look up at him. "And I
know too much discussion on babies or families
makes you shut down and get all misty-eyed, yet
you're a nanny."

Scarlett tightened her lips together and tried to
ignore that burn in her throat and eyes.

Beau slid his finger beneath her chin and tipped
her head up. "Shall I keep going?" he asked. "Or
maybe you could just tell me what you're running
from."

Scarlett pulled in a shaky breath and closed her
eyes. "I can't have children."

Eleven

Beau's suspicions were right. He wished like hell he'd been wrong because he could see the pain in her eyes, hear it in her voice.

Just as he started to reach for her again, she opened her eyes and held up one hand. "No. I don't need to be consoled and please, don't look at me like that."

He didn't know what she saw in his eyes, but how could he not comfort her? He may have the reputation of a playboy, and perhaps he didn't do anything to rectify that with the media, but he did care.

Even though he'd only known Scarlett a short time, it was impossible to ignore the way he felt.

Attraction was one thing, but there was more to this complex relationship.

Unfortunately, he had to ignore the pull and remain closed off from tapping into those unwanted, untimely feelings. He had a future to figure out and he'd already screwed up with one woman.

"I love being a nanny," she went on, her voice still laced with sadness and remorse. "But my life changed about a year ago, and I just can't do this job anymore."

"That's why you're leaving."

Beau crossed to the bed and sat down. Maybe she'd feel more apt to talk if he wasn't looming over her in only his underwear. He never wanted her to feel intimidated or insecure. He doubted she really had anyone she could talk to and the fact that she chose him—after he'd somewhat forced her hand—proved she was more vulnerable than he'd first thought.

But he actually wanted to listen and he wanted to know how he could help…even if that only came in the form of making her forget.

"I can't be in Stone River." Scarlett's words cut through his thoughts. "There are too many memories here of my life, my hopes and dreams. Starting over somewhere fresh will be the best healer for me."

He understood all too well about needing to start over. The need to find a place that would be comforting and not pull you down further. Her reasons for leaving Stone River were the exact reasons he'd left

LA. They both needed something new, something that promised hope for an unknown future.

"I'm sure that wasn't an easy decision to make," he stated.

She turned to face him and shrugged one slender shoulder. "There wasn't much else I could do. After my surgery, I took a position out of the field, in the office. I love the people I work with. I just couldn't be a nanny anymore. I thought working in the office would be easier, but it wasn't. I was still dealing with families and listening to the stories of my co-workers. Then Maggie asked me to fill in for these few weeks before I leave and I couldn't tell her no."

"I'm glad you didn't."

Scarlett stared at him for a minute. The lamp on her bedside table set a soft glow on her mocha skin. Skin he ached to touch again. Scarlett was one of the sexiest, most passionate women he'd ever known, and after hearing a bit of her story, he knew she was also one of the strongest.

"Me, too," she whispered.

He did reach for her now and when her hand closed in his, he pulled her toward him. Scarlett came to stand between his legs and she rested her hands on his shoulders.

"What surgery did you have to have?" he asked.

When she pulled in a shaky breath, he placed his hands on her waist and offered a comforting squeeze.

"I had a hysterectomy," she explained. "The short version of my story is I had a routine checkup. The test results came back showing I had some abnormal cells and the surgery was necessary. Unfortunately, that took away any chance I had at my own family, but in the end, the threat of uterine cancer was gone."

He couldn't imagine wanting something, dreaming of having it your whole life and then not obtaining it. There was nothing Beau didn't covet that he couldn't get through money or power. That's how he'd been raised. Yes, his parents had instilled in him a strong work ethic, but he also knew that at any given time he could reach for anything and make it his.

Yet with all his money, power and fame, he couldn't make his own future stable when he was so confused where he should land. And if he had the ability, he'd sure as hell do something to make Scarlett's life easier.

With a gentle tug, Beau had Scarlett tumbling onto his chest. He gripped her thighs and helped her straddle his lap. As he looked up into her eyes, he realized that if there was any woman who could make him lose his heart, it could be her.

Which was absolutely crazy. Why was he even having such thoughts? He'd screwed things up before when he'd let his heart get involved. Wanting a woman physically and thinking of deeper emotions were two totally different things and he needed to refocus before he found himself even further from where he needed to be.

Between all of this with his family and now his

mixed feelings for Scarlett, he needed to remain in control before he completely lost himself.

"Let's keep our painful pasts out of this room, out of this bed," he suggested as he nipped at her chin. "For as long as you're here, stay with me."

Her eyes widened as she eased slightly away. "You want to continue this fling?"

"'Fling'? That's such a crass word." He let his hands cover her backside and pull her tighter where he needed her most. "We don't need a title for this. Just know I want you, for however long you're here."

Scarlett laced her hands behind his neck and touched her forehead to his. "I swore I wouldn't do this with you," she murmured.

"Yet here we are."

She laughed, just as he'd hoped. "I guess I'm wearing too many clothes."

He stripped her shirt off, sliding his hands and eyes over her bare torso, her breasts. "Let's make each other forget."

Scarlett pushed Madelyn in the child swing that had been hung on the back patio. Even though winter had settled in and they were closing in on Christmas, the sun was shining bright in the cloudless sky and with a light jacket and pants, the day was absolutely beautiful.

Madelyn cooed and grinned as the swing went back and forth. Scarlett couldn't help but return the smile. It was impossible to be unhappy around Madelyn. Even when she'd fussed about her sore gums, Scarlett cherished the time. Madelyn was such a special little girl and having a father who cared so deeply made her very fortunate.

Beau had made a difficult decision to leave his Hollywood home and find out what life he and his daughter should lead.

Maybe he'd go back to his home in LA, but for now he seemed to be in no hurry. After spending the past several nights in his bed—well, hers—Scarlett wasn't in too big of a hurry to leave, either.

But she had to. She couldn't stay here forever playing house. There was no happily-ever-after for them, no little family. No, Scarlett wasn't going to get that family…at least not with Beau.

Maybe one day she'd meet a man and he might have kids already or maybe they'd adopt. She still couldn't let go of that dream. A new dream had replaced the old one and Scarlett had a blossom of hope.

Strong arms wrapped around her from behind, pulling her out of her thoughts, and Scarlett squealed.

"It's just me," Beau growled in her ear. "Unless you were expecting someone else."

Scarlett eyed him over her shoulder. "My other lover was supposed to come by because I thought you were out."

He smacked her butt. "There are no other lovers as long as I'm in your bed," he said with a smile.

Which would only be for another two weeks.

Scarlett didn't want to think of the end coming so soon. Only a few days ago she was counting down until she could hightail it out of town, but now...

Well, falling into bed with Beau had changed everything.

"I thought you were with Colt and Hayes looking over résumés for guides for the dude ranch."

The new business venture of the Elliott brothers was due to start in early spring. Scarlett had heard Beau discussing how much still needed to be done, she was only sorry she wouldn't be around to see how magnificent all of this would be. Pebblebrook was a gorgeous, picturesque spread and no doubt they would draw in thousands of people a year.

Scarlett wondered if Beau and Colt had told their dad about the ranch, about the way they were closing in on making his dream a full reality, when they'd gone to see him yesterday morning. But Beau had been closed off when he'd returned. Scarlett hadn't wanted to press him on a topic that was obviously so sensitive. She couldn't imagine that bond father and son had shared growing up and how much this must be hurting Beau.

Growing up, she did everything to avoid her stepfather and mom. They'd been so caught up in their own worlds anyway, so she went unnoticed.

"We finished early," Beau told her. "I told my brothers I needed to get back home to see Madelyn."

Scarlett gave the swing another gentle push and turned to face Beau. Those dark eyes, framed by thick lashes, all beneath a black brim only made him seem all the more mysterious. Over the last week she'd found out that there were several sides to him, and she had to admit she liked this Beau.

The man before her wasn't the actor she'd seen on-screen or the playboy the media portrayed. This Beau Elliott was a small-town rancher.

Albeit a billionaire.

She glanced over at Madelyn. "She woke from a nap about twenty minutes ago, so you're just in time."

Beau slid his hands up her arms, over the slope of her shoulders, and framed her face. "I may have wanted to see you, too."

Scarlett couldn't help the flutter in her chest. The more time she spent with him and his daughter, the more she realized how difficult leaving would be. But she'd be fine. She had to be.

"I also left because I have a surprise planned for you."

"A surprise?" she repeated, shocked he'd think to do anything for her. "What is it?"

Beau slid his lips softly over hers, then stroked her cheeks with the pad of his thumbs. "If I tell you then it won't be a surprise."

"Oh, come on," she begged. "You can't tease me like that."

He thrust his pelvis toward hers and smiled. "You weren't complaining about being teased last night, or the night before, or the night before that."

Scarlett slapped him on the chest. "Fine. But you'll pay for that."

Beau grazed his mouth along her jaw and up to the sensitive area just behind her ear. "I'm counting on it."

Madelyn let out a fuss, which quickly turned into a cry. Before Scarlett could get the baby from the swing, Beau had moved around her and was unbuckling her.

Scarlett stepped away and watched as he cooed and offered sweet words and patted her back. Something stirred inside her. An unfamiliar feeling. An undeniable feeling.

She was falling for Beau.

How ridiculous that sounded even inside her own mind. But there was no denying the fact. Beau Elliott had worked his way past her defenses and into her personal space, quite possibly her heart. There was no future here and she was a fool for allowing this to happen.

Of course she didn't *allow* anything. There had been no stopping these feelings. From the second Beau showed her just how selfless he was, how caring, Scarlett couldn't help but fall for him.

Beau lifted Madelyn over his head and spun in a circle. With the sun off in the distance and the soft rolling hills of the ranch as the backdrop, Scarlett had to tamp down her emotions. The father/daughter duo was picture perfect and maybe neither of them realized how lucky they were to have each other.

Scarlett let them have their moment as she slipped inside the tiny cabin. As silly as it was, she'd come to think of this little place like home. This was nothing like the massive home she'd grown up in. The place might as well have been a museum with the expensive furniture, priceless art and cold atmosphere.

Maybe that's why this cozy cabin touched her so much. There was life here, fun, a family. All the things she'd craved as a child and all the things she wanted as an adult.

But they weren't hers…and she needed to remember that.

Instead of dwelling on those thoughts, Scarlett moved to the kitchen where she'd baked sugar cookies earlier. They were ready to be iced and taken to Annabelle, Alexa and Pepper.

Scarlett didn't proclaim to be the best baker, but she did love her sugar cookie recipe. In fact, she'd made extra just for Beau. Maybe part of her wanted to impress him still, which was silly, but she hadn't been able to help herself. She cared for him, so much. Much more than she should be allowed.

The man came through the doorway just as her thoughts turned to him once again. Of course, he was never far from her thoughts, just as he was never far from her in this tiny space.

"I thought I smelled cookies when I came in earlier." He held Madelyn with one strong arm as he came to stand on the other side of the island. "But it looks as if you have enough to feed a small army. Are we expecting company?"

Scarlett started separating the icing she'd made into smaller bowls so she could dye it in different colors. "I'm taking a dozen each to your brothers' houses later. I just… I don't know. I thought I should do something and I love to bake. I think Christmas just demands the house smell like warm sugar and comfort."

She applied two drops of yellow food coloring into the icing for the star cookies, then she put green drops into another bowl for the tree cookies. The silence had her unsettled so she glanced up to find Beau staring at her with a look on his face she'd never seen before.

"What?" she asked, screwing the lids back on the small bottles of food coloring.

"You watch my baby all day, you cook, you decorate—"

"Don't call that tree in the corner decorating," she grumbled. "Maybe I baked because I need a chance to redeem myself."

He chuckled and shifted Madelyn around to sit on the bar and lean back against his chest. He kept one firm hand on her belly.

"The mantel is beautiful and way more than I'd ever think of doing, and the front porch looks like a real home with the wreath and whatever you did to that planter by the steps." He slid his hat off and dropped it onto a bar stool. "I don't know how you do it all. Maybe women are just born with that gene that makes them superhuman."

"We are."

His smile widened. "And a modesty gene, too, I see."

"Of course," she said without hesitation.

"Regardless of how you get everything done, I'm grateful."

The sincerity of his statement just pulled back another layer of defense she'd tried to wrap herself in. Unfortunately, every time the man opened his mouth, he stripped away more and more. She was losing this fight with herself and before these next couple of weeks were up, she had serious concerns about her heart.

"How long until the cookies are ready to deliver?" he asked.

"I just need to ice three dozen." She glanced behind her to the trays lining the small counter space. "I can ice the dozen for us after I get back."

"You made cookies for us, too?"

Scarlett laughed. "You think I'm baking and not thinking of myself?"

Madelyn let out a jumble of noises as she patted her father's hand. Was there anything sexier than a hunky rancher caring for his baby? Because she was having a difficult time thinking of anything.

"Well, as soon as you get those iced, you'll get your surprise," he told her. "This will all work out quite well."

"What will?"

"The deliveries, your surprise." He leaned in just a bit as his eyes darted to her mouth. "Coming back here later and pleasuring you."

Her body heated, not that she needed his promise for such a reaction. Simply thinking of him incited her arousal. But all of the emotions swirling around inside her were so much more than sexual. Her heart had gotten involved in this short span of time. She hadn't seen that coming. She'd been so worried about not falling for his seduction, she hadn't thought of falling for the man himself.

Damn it. She was sinking fast and not even trying to stop herself. Why bother? Why not just enjoy the ride as long as this lasted?

She deserved to go after what she wanted, no matter how temporary, and she wanted Beau Elliott. Considering he wanted her just as much, there was no reason to let worry in now.

For the time they had left, she planned on enjoying every single moment of her last job as a nanny.

As for her heart, well, it had been broken before. But she hadn't experienced anything like Beau Elliott. Would she ever be able to recover?

Twelve

Scarlett put the final lid on the gold Christmas tin. She stacked the festive containers in a tote and went to get Madelyn from her swing in the living room. Thankfully, she wasn't so fussy with her swollen gums now. The teething ring had helped.

"All ready?"

She turned to see Beau. "I'm ready." Giddiness and anxiousness spiraled through her. "Just what is this surprise?"

That familiar, naughty smile spread across his face. Beau could make her giddy like a teenager with her first crush and arouse her like a woman who knew exactly what she was getting into. She'd never met a man who could elicit such emotions from her.

"You're about to find out," he promised with a wink. "Let me take the cookies out and I'll be right back."

"I can carry them," she argued.

Beau put his hand up. "No. Stay right there with Madelyn. Actually, she'll need a jacket and hat. It's cool this evening and we'll be outside for a bit."

Scarlett narrowed her eyes. "We're not driving to your brothers' houses?"

The estate had a ridiculous amount of acreage—she thought she'd heard the number of five thousand thrown out—so the only way around the place was on tractors, four-wheelers, horses or cars.

With only a smile for her answer, Beau adjusted the wide brim of his black hat before he grabbed the bag stuffed with cookie tins and headed out the front door.

Scarlett glanced to Madelyn and tapped the tip of her nose.

"Your daddy is driving me crazy."

By the time Scarlett grabbed the jacket and hat for Madelyn from the peg by the door, Beau swept back inside.

"I'll finish getting her ready," he said, taking his daughter. "Take a jacket and hat for yourself, too. I can't have you shivering or you won't appreciate the surprise."

Scarlett laughed. "You're making me nervous, Beau."

He reached up and stroked one finger down the side of her face. "Trust me."

How could she not? She trusted him with her body...and he was closing in on her heart.

Scarlett smiled, mentally running from the unfamiliar emotions curling through her. "You know I do."

She went to her room to get her things. Whatever Beau had planned, he seemed pretty excited about what he'd come up with.

Warmth spread through her at the thought of him thinking of a way to surprise her. Was this a Christmas present or just because? Or did this surprise involve something he liked, as well? The questions and the unknowns were driving her crazy.

It was difficult not to read more into this situation because they'd agreed to have just these last couple of weeks of intimacy before she left. So why was he going that extra mile? Why was he treating this like...well, like a relationship?

Scarlett groaned as she tugged on her red knit hat. Her thoughts were trying to rob her happy time here. She had one of the sexiest men in the world waiting to give her something he'd planned just for her. And she'd simply enjoy it.

She slid on her matching red jacket, perfect for the holiday season and delivering Christmas cookies. For another added bit of flair, she grabbed her black-and-white snowflake scarf and knotted it around her neck.

When she stepped back into the living room, Beau held Madelyn in one hand and extended his other toward her. He kept that sneaky grin on his face and she just knew he was loving every minute of torturing her.

Giddy with anticipation, Scarlett slid her hand in his. She had to admit, she liked the look of her darker skin against his. Her bright red nails were quite the contrast with his rough fingertips from working on the ranch.

Beau tugged her forward until she fell against his side and he covered her mouth with his. The short yet heated kiss had her blinking up at him and wondering how he kept knocking her off her feet. She never knew what he'd do next, but he continued to have her wanting more.

"Everything's ready," he told her. "Go on outside."

She couldn't wait another second. Scarlett reached around him and opened the door. The moment her eyes focused on the sight before her, she blinked, wondering if this was a dream.

"Beau," she gasped. "What did you do?"

Directly in front of the porch were two chocolate-brown horses in front of a wide wooden sled. A sled decorated with garland and lights. On the seat she saw plaid blankets. There was evergreen garland wrapped around the reins, and the horses stood stoic and stared straight ahead as they waited for their orders.

Scarlett spun back around and threw her arms

around Beau, careful of how she sandwiched Madelyn in the middle.

"I can't believe you did this," she squealed. "How on earth did you manage it?"

Beau took her hand in his and led her to the sled. "I have my ways and that's all you need to know."

Scarlett didn't hesitate as she carefully climbed into the sled. Once she nestled against the cushioned seat, she reached down for Madelyn.

The sled jostled slightly as Beau stepped up into it and folded his long, lean frame next to her. He gripped the reins in hand as Scarlett pulled the cozy blanket up over their laps. She laced her hands around Madelyn and glanced to Beau as he snapped the reins to set the sled in motion.

"Why did you do all of this?" she asked.

"Why not?" he countered, shooting her that toe-curling grin and dark gaze. "You mentioned loving Christmas and sleigh rides. I'm just giving you a bit of extra cheer."

Scarlett wasn't quite sure what to say. Beau had put so much thought into this, even though he tried to brush the sweet gesture aside. This full-on reality was so much better than anything she'd ever seen in the movies.

"I'm glad I made you a dozen cookies, then," she joked as he headed in the direction of Nolan's house. "You may even get extra icing."

"Is that a euphemism?"

Scarlett's body heated, but she laughed because

she didn't want to get all hot and bothered when she was in the midst of this festive family moment.

The breath in her throat caught and was instantly replaced with thick emotions. Family. This fantasy moment she was living in had thrust her deeper into her job than she'd ever been.

Feeling like part of the family was often just a perk of being a nanny. But nothing had ever prepared her for falling for the man she worked for, or for his daughter. And how could she not fall for him? He'd been attentive since day one…which really wasn't all that long ago.

Still, Beau actually listened to her. He met her needs in the bedroom and out, and she was an absolute fool if she thought she'd walk away at the end of this without a broken heart.

"So you'll be leaving at the end of next week for your movie premiere," she stated, more reminding herself and making sure this stayed out in the open. "Are you sure you'll be home Christmas Eve?"

"Positive," he assured her. "Nobody else is playing Santa to my girl but me."

"I wondered if you'd bought presents."

He shot her a side glance. "Of course I have. You think I'd let my baby's first Christmas come and go and not have presents?"

"Well, you didn't have a tree or a stocking," she reminded him with an elbow to his side.

Beau guided the horses as Nolan's home came into view. The large log resort-type home looked like something from a magazine. Not surprising, though, since the Elliotts had the lifestyle of billionaire ranchers and Nolan was a surgeon. He and Pepper lived here with their little one and their home was beautifully decorated, with wreaths adorning every window and a larger one with a red bow on the front door.

"Maybe I didn't have a tree or stockings," Beau added. "But I'm not a complete Scrooge."

Scarlett shifted in the seat and glanced down at the baby. "I think we're putting her to sleep," she stated. "Next time her gums are bothering her, just hitch up the sled and take her for a ride."

"Sure." He snorted. "No problem."

Within another minute, Madelyn was fast asleep. There were so many questions Scarlett had for Beau regarding his future, but she wasn't sure if she had a right to ask…or if she even truly wanted to know the answers.

She decided to wait until they left Nolan's house to bring up her thoughts. Nolan and Pepper weren't home, so Beau left the tin on the porch swing and sent his brother a text.

As they took off again, this time toward Hayes and Alexa's house, Scarlett figured this was the perfect time. If he didn't want to answer, then he didn't have to, but she couldn't just keep guessing.

"When you go back for the movie premiere, do you think you'll want to stay?"

"No. I'll definitely be back here for Christmas."

Scarlett pulled the plaid blanket up a little further. "I mean, will being back there make you miss that life?"

He said nothing. Only the clomping of the horses through the lane broke the silence. Scarlett wondered if she'd gone too far, simply because he hadn't talked much about the movie and she got the impression that topic was off the table.

"Forget it," she said after waiting too long for his reply. "None of my concern. It's not like I'll be here or part of your life."

"It's okay." He shifted in his seat, his thigh rubbing against hers. "Honestly, I doubt it. I'm not looking forward to going back."

"Do you hate that world so much?"

Beau's brows dipped as he seemed to be weighing his words. "I hate how people can get so swept up in their own lives they forget there's a world around them. The selfishness runs rampant out there. Everyone is out for themselves, but they're never happy because when they get what they want, they still want more."

He pulled in a deep breath and shook his head. "I can say that because I'm that person."

Scarlett slid her left hand over Beau's denim-clad thigh. "You're not that person at all."

The muscles in his jaw clenched. "I am," he volleyed back. "I left here because I wanted more. I made it in Hollywood, had a career people would kill for and still wanted more. Then I won two big acting awards, and that wasn't enough, either. I met Jennifer and thought we might have had a future together, but that went to hell. I have a gorgeous baby, yet I'm still looking for more."

Scarlett didn't like the defeated tone in his voice. "You're not looking for more," she scolded. "You're looking for the right place to raise your daughter and trying to reconnect with your family. That's not selfish. And it sure as hell wasn't selfish that you surprised me with a horse-drawn sleigh ride."

"Oh, the sleigh ride was just so I'd get laid."

Scarlett squeezed his thigh until he yelped.

"I'm joking," he laughed. "Well, not really. I still want in your bed tonight."

"You didn't have to do this to get there," she reminded him. "I haven't been complaining, have I?"

He pulled back on the reins until the horses and sleigh came to a stop. When Beau shifted in his seat to face her, Scarlett's heart kicked up.

"I've been thinking…" He gripped the reins in one hand and slid his other beneath the blanket to cover hers. "I don't want to cheapen this to just sex or for you to ever think I'll forget you when you leave."

A burst of light filled the cracks in her heart. What exactly was he trying to say?

"I know you're moving and I have no idea where I'll be," he went on. "But I don't want to just hide in the cabin and keep you naked."

Scarlett rolled her eyes and glared. "Really?"

His lips quirked into a half grin. "Okay, that's

exactly what I'd like, but I want you to know you're more important to me than Madelyn's nanny or my temporary lover."

Scarlett pulled in a breath and held his dark gaze. "So what are you saying?"

"I want to take you on a date."

"A…a date?"

Not what she thought he'd say, but she wasn't exactly opposed to the idea.

"I didn't think you wanted to be seen in town or anywhere because of privacy."

He squeezed her hand and leaned forward to graze his lips across hers. There was no chill in the December air at all when she had Beau next to her. Just one simple touch, just one promised kiss had her entire body heating up.

When Beau eased back, he stroked the back of her hand with his fingertip. "Some things are worth the risk."

Well, that sealed the deal. There was no coming back from this because her heart tumbled, flipped, flopped, did all the amazing things that had her wanting to squeal and yell that she'd fallen completely in love with Beau Elliott.

Unfortunately, there was no room in this temporary relationship for such emotions. There would be no love, no family Christmas cards and definitely no happy-ever-after.

She only had a week left with Beau and then she'd be out of his life for good.

Thirteen

Beau wasn't sure what had made Scarlett shut down after he'd asked her on a date. Honestly, he hadn't planned on that impromptu invitation, but he'd needed her to know that she wasn't just some woman he'd seduced and conquered. He'd never thought of any woman in that manner, and he sure as hell had more respect for Scarlett than that.

She was special. Not because of how she cared for Madelyn and not because she was so easy to talk to. Scarlett presented the entire package of an honest woman, one who genuinely cared.

Part of him wanted to give her the world, but what part of his world could he actually give? He couldn't even figure out his own plan. Though after being at

Pebblebrook for a few weeks, he knew he wanted a ranch of his own. The hands-on approach he'd taken each day had turned something inside of him. The fact that he wasn't interested in looking at scripts now was rather telling.

Maybe one day he'd look to the screen again, but for now, Beau truly felt this was his destiny. He'd gone and explored like he'd wanted. He'd made himself one of the biggest names in Hollywood, but like he'd told Scarlett, something had still been missing.

Beau nearly laughed at himself for his *Wizard of Oz* epiphany. Everything he'd ever wanted was right here in his own backyard…literally.

He stood in front of the crazy Christmas tree in the corner of the cabin. Scarlett's soft singing voice filtered in from his bedroom as she got Madelyn to sleep for the night.

They'd delivered cookies and both Annabelle and Alexa were thrilled with the surprise. Beau loved the praise they gave Scarlett, and the fact that they treated her like family had him wanting to explore more with her. He'd never wanted someone like this before. Not just for sex, but to see if they could grow together.

But she was moving to Dallas.

Beau's mind raced in too many directions to try to keep up with, but he figured he didn't have a set place he wanted to be. He was quite literally free to do anything.

Was he even ready for something like this? He'd

come back home to mend relationships, not to try to build a new one. Added to that, he hadn't known Scarlett very long. Was he honestly considering this? He'd made such a terrible judgment call with Jennifer, but Scarlett was so different than his ex. Scarlett wasn't out to gain anything for herself or trying to use him for anything other than a job before she left.

As one idea formed into another, Beau found himself smiling while still staring at the undecorated tree—save for the lights.

"She's out."

Scarlett's words had him turning to face her. When he met her gaze across the room, she stopped and set the bottle on the kitchen island.

"What?" she asked, tipping her head. "You're smiling and you've been staring at my tree. You're plotting something, aren't you? Are we burning it and roasting marshmallows?"

Beau shook his head and circled the couch to head toward the kitchen. She never glanced away and he figured he looked like a complete moron because he couldn't wipe the smile off his face.

If she thought the sleigh ride was nice, she'd be utterly speechless when he presented her with the next surprise.

"We aren't burning it," he told her as he drew closer. "But in continuing your festive holiday cheer, I say we break out our cookies and get them iced."

She narrowed her dark eyes. "Why do I have a

feeling this will end with my clothes on the kitchen floor?"

Beau shrugged. "Because you're realistic."

Scarlett shook her head as she laughed. "You don't have to talk me into getting naked, you know?"

Beau slid his hands over the dip in her waist. "Maybe not, but I'm in the mood for dessert."

He backed her up until they circled the island. Scarlett gripped his biceps when she stumbled.

"What are you doing?" she asked, smiling up at him.

Beau planted a kiss on the tip of her nose. Her freakin' nose. Now he knew he'd gone and lost his mind. He'd never done such an endearing action before, but he couldn't help himself. For as sexy as Scarlett was, she was also quite adorable.

"We're going to ice those cookies," he told her. "You did promise."

She jerked back, her brows shooting up. "You seriously want to ice cookies? Does this mean I'm melting Scrooge's heart?"

He smacked her on the butt before releasing her. "I'm hardly Scrooge, but I'll admit I've never iced cookies. My mom did all of that. Baking and cookie decorating was serious business at Christmastime in my house and she wanted it to be perfect."

Beau grabbed the icing from the counter next to the stove and set it on the island. Then he reached back around for the tin of cookies.

"I guess Christmas baking was the one time she

wasn't about to let a bunch of boys ruin her creations." Beau glanced at the spread before him and laughed as he turned to Scarlett. "So I guess your work is cut out for you."

Scarlett went to pull off all of the lids, revealing the yellow, green and red food coloring. The instant smell of sugar hit him and he couldn't wait to take a bite.

Beau picked up a bare cookie and dipped it in the yellow icing before taking a bite. "You're right. These are good."

"Beau," she exclaimed, smacking his chest. "The icing isn't a dip."

He chewed his bite and went back in for more icing—red this time. "I think I'm onto something here."

"You're impossible." She reached into a drawer and pulled out a plastic spatula. "Let me show you how you should ice cookies."

As he continued to dip, Beau watched her expertly smooth the frosting over the tree cookie. When she was finished, she laid it aside on the wax paper and grabbed another.

"Want to try?" she asked.

"Sure."

He took the cookie and the utensil, then dipped the spatula into the red icing. With a quick move, he streaked a stripe across her shirt.

"Oops." He smiled and shrugged. "That didn't

work. You might want to take your shirt off before that stains."

Scarlett propped a hand on her hip and narrowed her eyes. "That's not very original."

He gave another swipe. "Maybe not, but I bet you take that shirt off."

She kept her eyes on his as her fingers went to the top button. One slow release at a time, she revealed her dark skin and festive red bra.

Once she dropped her shirt to the floor, she reached around him and picked up another cookie. She grabbed the spatula from his hand and proceeded to decorate.

"Just because you act childish doesn't mean the lesson is over," she informed him. "Do you see how I'm using nice, even strokes?"

"I can use even strokes, too."

Scarlett rolled her eyes and laughed. "I'm talking about icing."

Beau leaned in and nipped at her ear. "Maybe I was, too."

Scarlett leaned slightly into him. "I can't concentrate when you're doing that."

Good. He slid his hand along the small of her back, around the dip in her waist, and covered her flat abdomen. She shivered beneath his touch, just as he'd expected.

"I can't concentrate when you're not wearing a shirt," he whispered in her ear.

She tipped her head back to meet his gaze. "And whose fault is that?"

"You're the one who took it off."

Beau spun her slightly and gripped her hips. He lifted her onto the counter, away from the mess. "Let's see what else we can do with this icing."

Her eyes darkened as she raised a brow. "You didn't really want to learn how to decorate cookies, did you?"

He flashed her a smile. "Not at all."

But he did make use of all of the icing and by the end of the night, Scarlett wasn't complaining.

Scarlett lifted Madelyn out of the car seat and adjusted the red knit cap. Downtown Stone River may be small, but people bustled about and businesses thrived like in a major city.

The sun was high in the sky, shining down on this picturesque square. The large tower clock in the middle struck twelve. Benches in a circle around the clock were filled with couples eating lunch. Every single lamppost had garland and lights wrapped around it. Oversize pots sat on each corner and overflowed with evergreens and bright red poinsettias.

Scarlett would miss this place.

"Hey. You okay?"

Beau came to stand beside her, his hand resting on her back. She offered him a smile and nodded.

"I'm fine," she told him. "And ready to eat. I used too much energy last night."

"We could've had more cookies for breakfast," he offered with a naughty grin and a wink.

"Considering you ate every cookie and, um…we finished the icing, that wasn't an option."

Mercy, her body still tingled just thinking about what they had done with those colors. The extra-long shower to cleanse their bodies of the sticky mess had only led to even more intimacy. And more intimacy led to Scarlett wishing she didn't have to leave.

"I think we should try that café on the corner," he said, pointing over her shoulder. "It looks like you."

"I've eaten there before," she told him, without looking to see which place he referred to. "And what do you mean it looks like me?"

Beau shrugged and looked back down at her. His wide-brim hat shielded a portion of his face from the sun. She didn't know if he wore the hat because he'd gotten used to it since he'd been back or if he'd brought it to be a little discreet. Either way, he looked like the sexy cowboy she'd come to know and love.

Fine. There it was. The big L word she'd been dancing around and not fully coming to terms with. She knew she was falling, but she could admit now that she was there.

"It's all festive with the gold-and-red Christmas signs out front," he told her, oblivious to her thoughts. "The big wreath on the doorway, the candles in the windows. It just looks like you."

She figured that was a compliment, but she wasn't quite sure.

Madelyn let out a yawn and rubbed her eyes. Scarlett patted her back and eased her head down onto her shoulder.

"We should eat so we can get this one to take a nap on the car ride home," she told him.

Beau's cell went off and he groaned. "I'm not answering that."

"You should," she retorted. "It could be about your dad."

Which he'd still never talked about. She wanted to know his feelings and help him if she could. Maybe when they got back home she'd address the topic.

Beau pulled his cell from his pocket and stared at the screen, then a wide smile spread across his face.

"I take it that's not your agent?" she asked.

He pocketed the cell and leaned in, covering her mouth with his. The kiss ended as quickly as it started, leaving her a bit unbalanced.

"What was that for?" she asked.

"I have a surprise for you."

Her heart warmed. "Another one?"

"I promise, this one is much better than the last."

Scarlett's face lit up. "Tell me."

He kissed her once again, lingering a bit longer this time. "When we get home."

"Then we're getting our food to go."

Beau laughed as he steered her toward the café. "No, we're not. I promised you a date and that's what we're doing."

Fourteen

Scarlett wasn't sure whether to be nervous or not with Beau's mysterious surprise. They stepped into the cabin and Madelyn was wide-awake now after a brief nap in the car.

Beau had only been asked about twenty times at the café for his autograph, and with each person who approached him, he took the time to talk and sign. He might be a star, but he was also humble and so far removed from the celebrity she'd originally thought him to be.

Christmas was coming quickly and he'd be leaving in just a few days for his premiere. Their time together had been rocky at first, but then it had become an absolute fantasy. She'd never, ever gotten involved with someone she worked for. Beau had made that personal ethic impossible, though, and she wasn't the least bit sorry.

"Wait right there," he told her.

Scarlett stood in the living area and obeyed. She couldn't imagine what could top the horse-drawn sleigh, but she couldn't wait.

She took Madelyn to the little play mat on the floor. Carefully, Scarlett eased down to her knees and laid Madelyn beneath the arch where random plush animals swung back and forth. At the sight of them, she started kicking her feet and making adorable cooing noises.

Scarlett stood back up and smiled. She was seriously going to miss this sweet little nugget.

"Are you ready?"

She spun around and her smile widened as Beau came back in with his laptop. "I don't know what I'm ready for, but bring it."

He took a seat on a bar stool and patted the other one for her. Once his computer was up, he clicked through several screens before pulling up a page with several images of a beautiful old white farmhouse. There was a stone path leading up to the door, four gables on each side of the house, a pond in the back. The landscaping had to have been professional and there was even a white porch swing with colorful pillows. The entire place looked straight out of a magazine.

"If you like the outside, I can move on and show you the inside," he told her.

Scarlett gasped. "Beau, did you buy this?"

He clicked on the next screen and pulled up the entryway photo. "I knew it was the one the second my real estate agent sent options."

Joy consumed her and she reached for his hand. "Beau, I'm so happy for you. I didn't know you were that close to finding a permanent home."

She glanced back to the screen and looked at the thumbnail photos. "Click on that one," she said, pointing. "I think that will make a perfect room for Madelyn. Does it overlook the pond?"

"Wait." He squeezed her hand until she shifted her focus to him. "I bought this house for you."

Scarlett jerked back. "What? For me?"

He released her hand and clicked on another tab. "See? It's just outside of Dallas and only a twenty-minute commute to your new job."

Shock and denial replaced happiness. She stared at him for a moment before looking back to the image of the route from the new house to her new job. She didn't even know where to start with the questions because there were so many swirling around in her head.

"If you don't like it, I can put this on the market and find another," he went on.

She snapped her attention back to him. "Do you hear yourself? When people give gifts they usually give a scarf or a candle, sometimes jewelry. Who buys gift houses on a whim?"

Those dark brows drew in as if he were confused. "It wasn't necessarily a whim. I mean, I knew you were having trouble finding a place to live and I wanted to help you out. Besides, you've done so much for Madelyn and me, plus it's Christmas. I thought you'd like this."

Scarlett shook her head and slid off the stool. How in the world had this last job run the gamut of every single emotion she'd ever had? Worry, anxiety, stress, giddiness, love, anger…betrayal.

"You can't do this," she snapped as she turned back around. "You can't just send me on my way with a parting gift, as if that will replace what has happened here."

Damn it. She hadn't meant to let that sliver of her feelings out. She didn't want him to know how much she'd valued and cherished every second of their time together. When it was time for her to go, she'd have to make a clean break in an attempt to keep her heart intact…if that was even possible.

"You think that's what I'm doing?" he asked. "I bought this for you to make your transition easier, because you deserve a damn break. Why are you angry?"

Maybe her anger stemmed from confusion and hurt and the loss of a hope that maybe they could've been more. Which was ridiculous considering who he was, how they met and how little they'd known each other.

But still, how could she just ignore all that had transpired up until this moment? They'd shared a bed almost every night, he took her on a sleigh ride, he asked her on a date…they'd crammed a lifetime of memories into a few short weeks.

"I can't accept this gift," she told him. "I can't live in a house that you bought when you were thinking of me. When I leave here, I need to be done with what we had, and living there would only remind me of you. Besides, I couldn't accept something so extravagant. It's just not normal, Beau."

"It's not normal to want to help?" he tossed back. "Who's to say I wouldn't come visit?"

Oh, now that was just being cruel. "For what? To extend the affair? What happens if you meet someone else or I do? What happens when one of us decides to get married? We can't drag this affair on forever."

No, because that would be a relationship and they'd both agreed this fling was temporary. Besides, after she left, she didn't want to know who he was seeing or what was going on in his personal life. No doubt she'd see another piece of arm candy at his side. She certainly wouldn't follow him on social media, but his face would be on every tabloid at the supermarket checkout line. It would be difficult to dodge him completely.

Beau opened his mouth, but a pounding on the

cabin door stopped him. Scarlett propped her hands on her hips and stared at him across the room. More pounding on the door had Beau cursing.

He went to the door and jerked it open. "What?" he barked.

Colt stood on the other side holding his cell up for Beau to see a photo. Scarlett couldn't make out exactly what it was, but Beau's shoulders went rigid and he let out a string of curses.

"Want to explain what the hell this is?" Colt demanded. "I believed you when you said she was only your nanny."

Scarlett went nearer to see the image on the phone Colt held out. An image of Beau, Madelyn and Scarlett on the street earlier when he'd leaned in to kiss her. Above it was the headline: "A New Leading Lady for Hollywood's Favorite Cowboy."

Scarlett stilled. Was nothing sacred anymore? It just took one person to snap a picture on their phone and send it to the masses.

Colt's eyes went to her, then back to Beau.

"I am his nanny," Scarlett started. "We just—"

"It's not like that," Beau said, cutting her off. He kept his back to her and his focus on his brother. "She is my nanny and when I leave for the premiere, she'll stay here and care for Madelyn. Scarlett is moving next week and we went out for lunch. I leaned in and kissed her, so what? It's nobody's business."

"Nobody's business?" Colt roared as he pushed his way inside. "You do realize we are trying to honor our father and work on the opening of this dude ranch. Now you're back in town and making headlines like this. What about two weeks from now when it's another woman, or another? We're a close family, with strong core values Dad taught us. Those are the values we want to promote in this new business."

"Calm down," Beau demanded. "Scarlett and I kissed. Don't read anything more into that. It was an innocent kiss. I didn't think anything of it. The only person who will make a big deal about this is you."

Innocent kiss? He didn't think anything of it?

The air whooshed from her lungs and her throat clogged with emotions. She turned from the dueling brothers and went to Madelyn. Blinking against the tears gathering in her eyes, Scarlett bent down and lifted Madelyn in her arms. Then she headed toward her room.

"I'll let you two talk," she said without glancing their way.

She couldn't let Beau see her hurt. She couldn't let him see just how his words had cut her down. What happened to the man she'd come to know? To pretend their kisses meant nothing was flat out a bastard move.

So she'd hide out in her room and gather her strength. Because there was going to be a showdown and there was no way in hell she'd confront him with tears in her eyes.

Fifteen

"You better get your head on straight," Colt commanded through gritted teeth. "Scarlett isn't one of your random women."

Beau glanced to the closed bedroom door and wanted to punch something. He fisted his hands at his sides to prevent decking his own twin.

"I never said she was." Beau faced Colt and pulled in a deep breath. "I said this was nobody's business. And the dude ranch won't suffer because I kissed someone in public. Don't be so dramatic."

Colt adjusted his hat and pocketed his phone. "That's not what I'm saying. You claimed you've changed, but all of the media wrapped their claws around you and what woman you'd be with on any given day. I don't want that carried over here."

"It's not."

Damn it. He didn't want to have this conversation with Colt. He wanted to be in that bedroom because he knew he'd hurt Scarlett with his careless attitude. In his defense, he hadn't wanted to let Colt in on the relationship. He'd been trying to save her reputation. Instead, he'd left her thinking what they had wasn't special.

Only a jerk would purposely hurt a woman.

"If you're done berating me like a disappointed parent, you are free to go."

Colt clenched his jaw and nodded. "If you want to prove you've changed, then start by doing right with Scarlett."

His brother turned and left the cabin, closing the door with a hard click that echoed through the tiny space. Beau muttered a string of curses and raked his hand over the back of his neck. He should've seen this coming. One of the reasons he'd been staying in the cabin was because he'd wanted to dodge the press and any outsiders while he tried to find some semblance of normalcy.

Of course then Scarlett landed on his doorstep and everything snowballed from there. Somehow he needed to fix this—all of it. Her anger toward the home he'd purchased for her, hurting her and having Colt witness everything.

This morning he'd been full of hope and the possibility of exploring a future with her. Now…hell, he didn't have a clue what lay on the other side of that door.

Beau made his way across the cabin and tapped his knuckles on Scarlett's bedroom door. Without waiting for an answer, he tried the knob, surprised she hadn't locked him out.

Easing the door open, he peeked his head through. Scarlett sat cross-legged on her bed reading a book to Madelyn, who lay in front of her on the plaid quilt.

"What you heard out there—"

"Was the truth," Scarlett said as she closed the book and laid it on the bedside table. "You didn't say anything but the truth. There's nothing more to us than a few weeks of passion and a good time. We've made memories, but that's where it ends."

Beau slipped into her room, but remained by the open door. Her words shocked him. Her steely demeanor seemed so out of character, and he wasn't sure what to say.

Scarlett swung her legs off the side of her bed and came to her feet. She made sure to keep distance between them.

"Since we are so close to the end of our time together," she said, "it's probably best to end the intimate side of things. I'm sure you understand why. And I'm sure you can see why I cannot accept the house. I appreciate the gesture, but you should have your agent put it back on the market."

Well, wasn't her speech all neat and tidy and delivered with an iciness he never expected from someone so warm and caring.

Beau had never experienced this before. Rejection. But it wasn't the rejection that stung. No, what really sliced him deep was the fact that he had caused Scarlett so much suffering that she'd resorted to this as her defensive mechanism.

"Maybe I'm not ready to end things," he stated, folding his arms over his chest.

She stared at him across the room and finally took a step toward him. "There's no reason to prolong this, Beau. I will continue to care for Madelyn and watch her while you're gone to your premiere. But Maggie will be back next week and I'll be gone. This had to come to an end sometime."

Beau couldn't penetrate this wall she'd put up so quickly around herself. She'd need time and he needed to respect her enough to give it to her. Unfortunately, time wasn't on their side. He could give her today, but that's all he could afford.

"Scarlett, I never want you to believe that kiss, and everything before that, meant nothing." He needed her to know this above all else. "Anything I said to Colt was to protect you. Maybe I didn't go about it the right way, but don't think that I don't care for you."

Scarlett crossed her arms over her chest and nodded. "I'm going to feed Madelyn and take her for a walk to the stables. Then I'll come back and fix dinner."

She didn't extend the invite to the stables. Beau would stay behind, to give her time to think. Because there was no way she could just turn off this switch. If she felt half of what he felt for her, she couldn't ignore such strong emotions.

"I'll make dinner," he volunteered.

"Fine." She reached down and lifted Madelyn in her arms. "If you'll take her for a minute, I need to change my clothes."

"Scarlett—"

"Please."

Her plea came out on a cracked voice and he finally saw a sheen of tears in her eyes. She was struggling to hold everything together.

Beau reached for his baby and held her tight against his chest. Scarlett continued to stare at him, blinking against her unshed tears.

Without another word, he turned and left her alone in her room. After he shut the door firmly behind him, Beau went to his own room to contact his agent.

Not his real estate agent about the house. No, Beau had every intention on keeping that.

He laid Madelyn down in her crib and handed her a plush toy to chew on. With a deep sigh and heavy dose of guilt, he pulled his cell from his pocket and dialed his agent.

"Beau," he answered. "You're one hell of a hard man to get ahold of."

There wasn't much to say and this conversation

was long, long overdue. But it was time for some changes and they were going to start right now.

Beau gripped the phone as he watched his daughter play.

"We need to talk."

Scarlett didn't know what was more difficult, having Beau in the cabin or knowing he was miles away and gearing up for a fancy movie premiere tomorrow.

The past few days had been strained, to say the least. They'd been cordial to each other, like strangers who were stranded together and forced to cohabitate.

Scarlett had just put Madelyn down for her morning nap and was heading to the sink to wash bottles when a knock sounded on the front door.

She wore only leggings and an oversize sweatshirt, and her hair was in a ponytail—compliments of insomnia, anxiety, and a broken heart. But she ignored her state of dress and went to see who the unexpected visitor was.

After glancing through the peephole, Scarlett pulled in a long, slow breath and blew it out before flicking the dead bolt and opening the door.

"Annabelle," she greeted. "What brings you by?"

His beautiful sister-in-law offered a sweet smile and held up a basket. "I brought fresh cranberry apple muffins. Can I come in?"

"I would've let you in without the bribe, but I

won't turn it down." Scarlett laughed as she stepped aside to let Colt's wife in.

Annabelle set the basket down on the island. "The muffins were just an excuse," she said as she turned back to face Scarlett. "Can we talk for a minute?"

Scarlett didn't know why Annabelle wanted to talk, but she wasn't stupid. Likely this had to do with Colt and Beau, but if the woman thought Scarlett had any hold over Beau or could sway him to work on the relationship with his brother, well, that couldn't be further from the truth.

"Sure," Scarlett replied. "Have a seat."

She hadn't seen or talked to any of Beau's family since Beau had left a couple of days ago. Scarlett didn't think Beau counted their kisses as nothing, but hearing the words had hurt just the same. And hearing those words only gave her the smack of reality that she'd needed in order to see that this wasn't normal. What normal, everyday woman fell in love with a movie star and had him reciprocate those feelings? The idea was simply absurd.

Annabelle took a seat on the leather sofa and Scarlett sat on the other end. "What's up?" Scarlett asked.

"I'm going to cut out the small talk because it's pointless." Annabelle crossed her legs and leveled her gaze at Scarlett. "I know you have feelings for Beau. Don't deny it. I saw the two of you together. And I can also tell you that he has feelings, too."

Scarlett wanted to deny both statements, but she

simply didn't have the energy. Maybe if she let Anna-belle talk, she'd get this off her chest and then leave. Scarlett preferred to sulk in private.

"I also know my stubborn husband came down pretty hard on Beau and you, by default," Annabelle went on. "This ranch is absolutely everything to him and he sometimes speaks before he thinks."

Scarlett smiled. "You didn't have to come down here to apologize for him."

"I'm not," Annabelle corrected. "He needs to apologize on his own. I'm here to tell you that you need to ignore what Colt says, what the media spec-ulate and what you're afraid of."

She let out a soft sigh as she scooted over a bit farther. "What I'm trying to say is, your time here is almost up and I'd hate for you to go when you have so much unresolved."

Scarlett glanced down to her clasped hands and swallowed. "How do you know what's unresolved?"

Annabelle reached over and offered a gentle squeeze of her hand. "Because Colt and Hayes com-mented on Beau's broodiness before he left for LA and he was so happy before that. You make him happy. When he came back here he was broken and scared. He'd never admit that, so don't tell him I said it. But he was so worried for Madelyn and how his relationships with his brothers would pan out…or even if they would."

Scarlett glanced back up. "Beau and I aren't anything. I mean, I won't lie and say things didn't progress beyond a working relationship, but that's over."

"Is it?"

Nodding, Scarlett chewed the inside of her cheek before continuing. "He hasn't fully let me in. I know about the reasons he left here when he was eighteen. I know the issues with his brothers and his dad. But when he and Colt went to see their dad the other day, Beau shut down and wouldn't let me help. I don't even know what happened."

Annabelle leaned back on the couch and released Scarlett's hands. "Grant didn't remember his sons," she stated. "Colt said Beau took it pretty hard and wouldn't even talk to him on the ride home."

Oh, Beau.

"He has let you in," Annabelle went on. "And I'm here to tell you that if you want to give it a try with him, I'm going to help. Alexa and Pepper are ready to join in, too."

Stunned, Scarlett eased back and laughed. "Excuse me?"

Annabelle's smile spread wide across her face. "We all three figured if you want to make a statement, it's going to have to be bold."

"The three of you discussed this?" Scarlett asked, still shocked. "What do you all think I should be doing?"

That smile turned positively mischievous and the

gleam in her eye was a bit disconcerting. Annabelle reached for her hand once again.

"What do you say about going to your first movie premiere?"

Sixteen

This entire thing was absurd. The fact that she'd let Annabelle, Alexa and Pepper not only talk her into using the Elliotts' private jet to fly to LA, but they'd given her a makeover on top of that. Somehow, in a whirlwind of deciding she couldn't let Beau go without a fight and getting her hair curled and lips painted, she'd ended up at a Hollywood movie premiere.

Scarlett sat in the back of a limo—somehow the dynamic trio managed to get her that as well—and looked over at Madelyn in the carrier car seat. She'd guarantee this was the only limo arriving tonight with a car seat in the back.

Somehow the ladies had not only procured a dress

for Scarlett, along with shoes and a fashionable bag, they'd found a red sparkly dress and matching head-band for Madelyn.

As the limo slowed, Scarlett turned her attention to the tinted window. Bright lights flooded the night, cameras flashed, the roar of the crowd filtered in and nerves swirled through her belly at the sight and sound.

What was she thinking coming here? She was so far out of her element. She didn't do crowds or glam or dressing up in a fitted, sequined emerald green gown with her hair curled and in bright red lipstick. She was more of a relaxed kind of girl who made homemade baby food and decorated with clearance Christmas decor.

"Ma'am, I'm going to pull closer to the red car-pet entrance," the driver informed her. "Please wait until a guard opens your door and escorts you out."

Oh, mercy. She was really going through with this. Scarlett didn't know how the incredible Elliott women managed the jet, the wardrobe, the limo and a last-minute invite to the red carpet to arrive just after Beau's car. No doubt money talked and they had tapped into some powerful resources to make all of this happen in less than twenty-four hours.

The car came to a stop and Scarlett unfastened a sleepy baby from her car seat. She cradled Madelyn against her chest and adjusted the headband, which had slipped down over one eye like a pirate's patch.

"You'll just be around the block?" she asked the

driver. "I'm leaving the rest of Madelyn's things in here."

"Yes, ma'am. You call me and I'll be right back. I'm only driving for you tonight."

Scarlett's stylish clutch was just large enough for a couple of diapers, a travel pack of wipes, her cell and her wallet. She'd just fed the baby before Madelyn fell asleep so they should be good for a few hours. Besides, who's to say Beau wouldn't publicly reject her and she'd be right back in this car in just a few moments?

But what if he asked her to stay? What if he wanted to take her and Madelyn into the premiere and whatever party after?

She'd worry about that when the time came. Right now, her car had eased up and came to another stop. The lights and the screams intensified and Scarlett had to concentrate on the sweet child in her arms, still sleeping and oblivious to this milestone moment.

The door opened and the warm California air hit her. She already missed Texas and the laid-back life with cool evenings. Maybe city life wasn't for her. Maybe she hadn't only found the man—she'd found a piece of herself that clicked right into place. Perhaps the next chapter she was going to start was the wrong one. She had so many questions…and they were all about to be answered.

Scarlett laid a protective hand over Madelyn's ears to protect her from the thundering noise, but she stirred and her eyes popped open.

Questions and microphones were shot in her direction, but Scarlett looked ahead, beyond the men in black suits with mics attached to their lapels. She ignored the questions of who she was, what part she had in the film, who was the cute baby.

Scarlett spotted a flash of the wide, familiar grin then broad shoulders eased away from one set of reporters to another. Beau was flanked by those men in suits who were unsmiling and whose eyes were always scanning the area.

A hand slid over her elbow and Scarlett jerked to see who was beside her.

"Right this way, ma'am." One of the suited men clearly recognized the newbie on the red carpet and tried to usher her along. "There is extra security tonight with all the hype. I'll make sure you and your little one get to the entrance of the theater."

She had to strain to hear him over the white noise of the crowd and she didn't even bother to tell him this child wasn't hers, but rather belonged to the star of the premiere. Had she made a mistake bringing Madelyn? Would Beau be upset? She wanted to show him they could all be a family—they could be one unit and build something solid together.

One thing she knew for certain: she wasn't about to stop and talk to the different media outlets. For one thing, she had nothing to say that she'd want printed or quoted. For another, she was here for only one reason and it wasn't to be interviewed.

Scarlett shifted Madelyn in her arms, still shielding the baby's ears from the chaos. She leaned toward the security guard as she tried to keep up with the pace he'd set.

"I don't need to talk to any reporters. I'm here with Mr. Elliott," she informed him. Then she realized how stalker-like that sounded, so she quickly added, "And this is his baby."

The guard looked at her then down to Madelyn, but Scarlett smiled, hoping he'd move this process along. She had a right to be here—she assumed since Annabelle assured her this was okay—and she couldn't wait.

The man finally nodded and gripped his lapel as he talked out the side of his mouth and ordered the guards up ahead to stop Beau from moving to the next set of reporters.

Scarlett pushed through, ignoring the yells from either side of the roped-off area. If she tried to take in all the lights, all of the questions, all of the chaos around her, she would give in to the fear and the anxiety that had accompanied her all the way from Texas.

She never should have let Beau walk out of that cabin thinking he didn't mean more to her. Their time together since she'd shut down had been so strained and she'd ached for him in ways she'd never imagined possible.

In her defense, she'd been hurt and thought it best if they made a clean break since their temporary arrangement was coming to an end anyway. Unfortunately, that clean break didn't work.

Because she loved him.

There was no way to ignore such strong emotions and if she had to make a fool of herself and take the biggest risk of her life, then she was willing to try for the man she'd fallen for so helplessly.

One of the escorts next to Beau tapped on his shoulder and intervened, pulling him from a current interview. Then the man leaned in and told Beau something that had Beau darting his gaze straight in her direction and their eyes instantly locked.

Scarlett wasn't sure if it was the shock in his eyes or the wide smile on his face that had her nerves kicking in even more. She watched as he raked that sultry dark gaze over her body. Even at this distance and despite the chaos around them, the visual lick Beau gave her had her body instantly responding.

His eyes snapped back to hers and then he was taking long strides to come back down the red carpet. Scarlett didn't think she'd ever seen him smile this much.

"Scarlett."

Beau reached her and shook his head, as if still processing what she was doing here. That went for her, too. She felt as if this whole night was surreal.

"How did you… What… Annabelle texted me and asked if I could get a couple of passes and a limo. My agent pulled everything together, but I just assumed she and Colt were coming."

Well, that explained how the quick red carpet treatment happened.

"Mr. Elliott, who's the lady?"

"Beau, is that your little girl?"

"Is Jennifer James no longer part of your life?"

Reporters shot off so many questions, so prying and so demanding. Part of Scarlett wished she would've waited until he got home, but the other part was glad she'd allowed herself to be talked into coming. Standing here, supporting him, was the only way she knew to truly show him how sorry she was and how much he meant to her.

"I wanted to surprise you," Scarlett told him. "This wasn't my idea, but I needed to tell you—"

He slid his hands up her bare arms and stepped farther into her, with Madelyn nestled between them.

"Say it," he demanded. "I need to hear it."

Scarlett stared up into those dark eyes. "What do you need to hear?"

"That you love me." A corner of his mouth quirked into a grin. "That's why you're here, isn't it?"

She shifted Madelyn, but Beau ended up easing his daughter up into his arms. He palmed her back with one large hand and held her secure against his chest.

Questions roared even louder, but his eyes never left Scarlett's. The media might as well not even exist; all his attention was on her.

How did she ever think that his words weren't genuine? That he didn't think they were something special? He'd shown her over and over again just how much she meant to him and she'd shied away in fear. She firmly believed that everything he told Colt was to save her reputation, which only added another layer of respect and love.

"Scarlett."

She smoothed her hand down her emerald beaded gown and tucked the clutch beneath her arm.

"I wanted to be the one to tell you." Scarlett smiled, though her nerves were at an all-time high. "But you stole the words from my mouth."

Beau's hand went to her hip and he leaned down. If she thought the crowd was loud before, that was nothing compared to the roar now. They were yelling so much. She couldn't make out full questions, but she did pick up on "romance" and "love." Yes, they had all of that and so much more.

"Say it," he told her again.

Her eyes darted away, but he raised his hand to cup her face, drawing her attention back to him.

"I'm right here," he stated. "They don't exist. It's just the three of us."

His sweet girl was a package deal and she absolutely loved how he always put Madelyn first. And she wanted them as a package because she couldn't think of a better present.

"I love you," she told him as she reached up to lay her hand over his. "I'm sorry I didn't have the courage to say it before, but I got scared the other day. All of this happened so fast, but everything I feel is so, so real."

He closed the distance between them and touched his lips to hers. And that set the media into a tizzy.

"Beau, is this your new leading lady from the picture?"

"Does she have a name?"

"Is this the rumored nanny?"

"Are you planning a Christmas proposal?"

Beau pressed his forehead to hers. "Are you sure you're ready for all of this tonight?"

Scarlett wasn't sure, but if this was what Beau's life consisted of, she'd find a way to make things work.

"If you love me, then I'm ready for anything," she said, easing back to glance up at him.

"I love you, Scarlett. As crazy as it is, as little time as we've known each other, I love you more than I ever thought I could love any woman."

Her heart swelled and she knew the risk she'd taken had paid off.

"I know I could've waited for you to get back to Texas, but Annabelle thought I should make a statement."

Beau chuckled as he slid an arm around her waist. "Baby, that dress is quite the statement and I plan on showing you when we get back to my place tonight."

She hadn't thought that far, but the idea of ending the night at his house in the Hollywood Hills, of seeing even more into his world had her giddy with anticipation.

Scarlett smoothed a hand over Madelyn's dark curls. "You mentioned wanting a big family and you know that I can't give you that."

"Adoption," he said, using one simple word to put her worries at ease and further prove just how amazing he was. "We'll have that large family when the time is right."

She chewed on her bottom lip and then smiled. "Is it too late to tell you that the farmhouse you bought is perfect for us?"

Beau tapped her forehead with a quick kiss. "That place was always for us," he explained. "I just didn't get a chance to tell you before Colt showed up and then you kicked me out of your room."

He'd planned that house to be for the three of them all this time? Scarlett's eyes welled with tears, but she couldn't cry. It had taken a small army to get this makeup so perfect.

"I think we need to give the reporters something to chew on before they break the barriers."

Scarlett nodded. "Whatever you think."

Beau cradled Madelyn in one arm and kept his other firmly around Scarlett's waist. He angled them toward the front of the red carpet so both sides of the aisle could see them. As soon as they were facing forward, the crowd seemed to hush, waiting for that next golden kernel of a story.

"I'm happy to announce that Scarlett Patterson is

in fact my next leading lady," Beau declared. "And my future wife."

Wife? Scarlett jerked her gaze to his, which warranted her a toe-curling wink that set butterflies fluttering in her stomach.

"Is that a proposal?" she asked, shocked her voice was strong.

Beau kept that wide grin on his face. "What do you say? Be my leading lady for life, Scarlett."

"Yes." As if any other answer was an option. "There's nobody else I'd ever want for the star in my life."

Flashes went off, one after another, causing a strobe light effect. As people started yelling more questions, Beau waved and smiled. Scarlett wasn't sure what world she'd stepped into, but the strong man at her side would help her through.

She never thought she'd have the title of leading lady, but as Beau escorted her into the venue, Scarlett realized there was no greater role she could think of—besides wife and mother, of course.

Once inside, Beau ushered her down a hallway to find some privacy.

"I'm taking a break from Hollywood," he told her when they stopped in a quiet place. "I decided that before you came, but now that I see a better future, I'm not sure I'll want to come back here at all."

She didn't know how to respond, but she didn't get a chance. Beau backed her up a step until she came in contact with the wall. He held Madelyn in one arm and reached up with his free hand to stroke the side of her face, then sifted his fingers through her hair.

"You take my breath away, Scarlett. I want you forever, so if we need to take things slow before we marry, I'll do whatever you want."

He kissed her, pouring out his promise and love. When he eased back, he kept his lips barely a whisper away.

"This is the greatest Christmas present I could have ever asked for," he told her.

Scarlett rested her hand over his on Madelyn's back. "Me, too, but I don't know what to wrap up and put beneath our crooked tree."

He nipped at her bottom lip. "How about more of that cookie dip?"

She wrapped her arm around his waist and smiled. "I think I can manage that, but first we have a movie premiere to get to."

"And then we have the rest of our lives to plan."

Epilogue

"**W**hat the hell is that?" Colt demanded.

Scarlett smiled and held up her hands in an exaggerated fashion toward the tree. "It's our Christmas tree," she exclaimed.

"Why is it crooked?"

Beau stepped into the room after putting Madelyn down for the night. "Don't ask. Just go with it."

Scarlett rolled her eyes. "He loves it, don't let him fool you."

Colt's brows drew in before he shook his head and shrugged. "Whatever makes you two happy."

Oh, she was most definitely happy. Christmas Eve was magical here at the ranch and tomorrow was Christmas where all of the Elliotts—spouses, fiancées, and children—would gather and start a new chapter.

"I just wanted to come by and let you guys know that I spoke with the nursing home and they're okay with us bringing Dad home for the day tomorrow."

Beau's eyes went from his brother to Scarlett, then back again. "Seriously?"

Colt nodded. "They said as long as he's having a good day. They offered to send a nurse, but I truly think once he's home, he might see something that triggers some memories, and we can care for him well enough. Even if he's only there an hour. I think we all need it."

Scarlett's heart swelled as tears pricked her eyes. She crossed the room to Beau and wrapped an arm around him.

"This is great news for you guys," she stated. "I think it's exactly what this family needs for a fresh start."

"I just hope he remembers," Beau added.

Colt nodded. "I have a feeling he will. I think this is definitely a Christmas for miracles."

He drifted his gaze toward the leaning tree. "I mean, if you can call that a Christmas tree, I think anything is possible."

Beau laughed as he hugged Scarlett tighter against him. "That tree embodies our lives. We're not perfect, but we're sure as hell trying."

Scarlett smiled as she watched the twins share an

unspoken message with their eyes and their matching grins.

Yes, this was a season for miracles.

* * * * *

In her brand-new series, New York Times
*bestselling author Brenda Jackson welcomes you
to Catalina Cove, where even the biggest
heartbreaks can be healed...*

Turn the page for a sneak peek at
Love in Catalina Cove

CHAPTER ONE

New York City

VASHTI ALCINDOR SHOULD be celebrating. After all, the official letter she'd just read declared her divorce final, which meant her three-year marriage to Scott Zimmons was over. Definitely done with. As far as she was concerned the marriage had lasted two years too long. She wouldn't count that first year since she'd been too in love to dwell on Scott's imperfections. Truth be told there were many that she'd deliberately overlooked. She'd been so determined to have that happily-ever-after that she honestly believed she could put up with anything.

But reality soon crept into the world of make-believe, and she discovered she truly couldn't. Her husband was a compulsive liar who could look you right in the eyes and lie with a straight face. She didn't want to count the number of times she'd caught him in the act. When she couldn't take the deceptions any longer she had packed her things and left. When her aunt Shelby died five months later, Scott felt entitled to half of the inheritance Vashti received in the will.

It was then that Vashti had hired one of the best divorce attorneys in New York, and within six weeks his private investigator had uncovered Scott's scandalous activities. Namely, his past and present affair with his boss's wife. Vashti hadn't wasted any time making Scott aware that she was not only privy to this information, but had photographs and videos to prove it.

Knowing she wouldn't hesitate to expose him as the lowlife that he was, Scott had agreed to an uncontested divorce and walked away with nothing. The letter she'd just read was documented proof that he would do just about anything to hold on to his cushy Wall Street job.

Her cell phone ringing snagged her attention, the ringtone belonging to her childhood friend and present Realtor, Bryce Witherspoon. Vashti clicked on her phone as she sat down at her kitchen table with her evening cup of tea. "Hey, girl, I hope you're calling with good news."

Bryce chuckled. "I am. Someone from the Barnes Group from California was here today and—"

"California?"

"Yes. They're a group of developers that's been trying to acquire land in the cove for years. They made you an unbelievably fantastic offer for Shelby by the Sea."

Vashti let out a loud shout of joy. She couldn't believe she'd been lucky enough to get rid of both her ex-husband and her aunt's property in the same day.

"Don't get excited yet. We might have problems," Bryce said.

Vashti frowned. "What kind of problems?"

"The developers want to tear down your aunt's bed-and-breakfast and—"

"Tear it down?" Vashti felt a soft kick in her stomach. Selling her aunt's bed-and-breakfast was one thing, having it demolished was another. "Why would they want to tear it down?"

"They aren't interested in the building, Vash. They want the eighty-five acres it sits on. Who wouldn't with the Gulf of Mexico in its backyard? I told you it would be a quick sale."

Vashti had known someone would find Shelby by the Sea a lucrative investment but she'd hoped somehow the inn would survive. With repairs it could be good as new. "What do they want to build there instead?"

"A luxury tennis resort."

Vashti nodded. "How much are they offering?" she asked, taking a sip of her tea.

"Ten million."

Vashti nearly choked. "Ten million dollars? That's nearly double what I was asking for."

"Yes, but the developers are eyeing the land next

to it, as well. I think they're hoping that one day Reid Lacroix will cave and sell his property. When he does, the developers will pounce on the opportunity to get their hands on it and build that golf resort they've been trying to put there for years. Getting your land will put their foot in the door so to speak."

Vashti took another sip of her tea. "What other problems are there?"

"This one is big. Mayor Proctor got wind of their offer and figured you might sell. He's calling a meeting."

"A meeting?"

"Yes, of the Catalina Cove zoning board. Although they can't stop you from selling the inn, they plan to block the buyer from bringing a tennis resort in here. The city ordinance calls for the zoning board to approve all new construction. This won't be the first time developers wanted to come into the cove and build something the city planners reject. Remember years ago when that developer wanted to buy land on the east end to build that huge shopping mall? The zoning board stopped it. They're determined that nothing in Catalina Cove changes."

"Well, it should change." As far as Vashti was concerned it was time for Mayor Proctor to get voted out. He had been mayor for over thirty years. When Vashti had left Catalina Cove for college fourteen years ago, developers had been trying to buy up the land for a number of progressive projects. The people of Catalina Cove were the least open-minded group she knew.

Vashti loved living in New York City where things were constantly changing and people embraced those changes. At eighteen she had arrived in the city to attend New York University and remained after getting a job with a major hotel chain. She had worked her way up to her six-figure salary as a hotel executive. At thirty-two she considered it her dream job. That wasn't bad for someone who started out working the concierge desk.

"Unless the Barnes Group can build whatever they want without any restrictions, there won't be a deal for us."

Vashti didn't like the sound of that. Ten million was ten million no matter how you looked at it. "Although I wouldn't want them to tear down Shelby, I think my aunt would understand my decision to do what's best for me." And the way Vashti saw it, ten million dollars was definitely what would be best for her.

"Do you really think she would want you to tear down the inn? She loved that place."

Vashti knew more than anyone how much Shelby by the Sea had meant to her aunt. It had become her life. "Aunt Shelby knew there was no way I would ever move back to Catalina Cove after what happened. Mom and Dad even moved away. There's no connection for me to Catalina Cove."

"Hey, wait a minute, Vash. I'm still here."

Vashti smiled, remembering how her childhood friend had stuck with her through thick and thin. "Yes, you're still there, which makes me think you need your head examined for not moving away when you could have."

"I love Catalina Cove. It's my home and need I remind you that for eighteen years it was yours, too."

"Don't remind me."

"Look, I know why you feel that way, Vash, but are you going to let that one incident make you have ill feelings about the town forever?"

"It was more than an incident, Bryce, and you know it." For Vashti, having a baby out of wedlock at sixteen had been a lot more than an incident. For her it had been a life changer. She had discovered who her real friends were during that time. Even now she would occasionally wonder how different things might have been had her child lived instead of died at birth.

"Sorry, bad choice of words," Bryce said, with regret in her voice.

"No worries. That was sixteen years ago." No need to tell Bryce that on occasion she allowed her mind to wander to that period of her life and often grieved for the child she'd lost. She had wanted children and Scott had promised they would start a family one day. That had been another lie.

"Tell me what I need to do to beat the rezoning board on this, Bryce," Vashti said, her mind made up.

"Unfortunately, to have any substantial input, you

need to meet with the board in person. I think it will be beneficial if the developers make an appearance, as well. According to their representative, they're willing to throw in a few perks that the cove might find advantageous."

"What kind of perks?"

"Free membership to the resort's clubhouse for the first year, as well as free tennis lessons for the kids for a limited time. It will also bring a new employer to town, which means new jobs. Maybe if they were to get support from the townsfolk, the board would be more willing to listen."

"What do you think are our chances?"

"To be honest, even with all that, it's a long shot. Reid Lacroix is on the board and he still detests change. He's still the wealthiest person in town, too, and has a lot of clout."

"Then why waste my and the potential buyer's time?"

"There's a slim chance time won't be wasted. K-Gee is on the zoning board and he always liked you in school. He's one of the few progressive members on the board and the youngest. Maybe he'll help sway the others."

Vashti smiled. Yes, K-Gee had liked her but he'd liked Bryce even more and they both knew it. His real name was Kaegan Chambray. He was part of the Pointe-au-Chien Native American tribe and his family's ties to the cove and surrounding bayou went back generations, before the first American settlers.

Although K-Gee was two years older than Vashti and Bryce, they'd hung together while growing up. When Vashti had returned to town after losing her baby, K-Gee would walk Vashti and Bryce home from school every day. Even though Bryce never said, Vashti suspected something happened between Bryce and K-Gee during the time Vashti was away at that unwed home in Arkansas.

"When did K-Gee move back to Catalina Cove, Bryce?"

"Almost two years ago to help out his mom and to take over his family's seafood supply business when his father died. His mother passed away last year. And before you ask why I didn't tell you, Vash, you know why. You never wanted to hear any news regarding what was happening in Catalina Cove."

No, she hadn't, but anything having to do with K-Gee wasn't just town news. Bryce should have known that. "I'm sorry to hear about his parents. I really am. I'm surprised he's on the zoning board."

For years the townsfolk of the cove had never recognized members of the Pointe-au-Chien Native American tribe who lived on the east side of the bayou. Except for when it was time to pay city taxes. With K-Gee on the zoning board that meant change was possible in Catalina Cove after all.

"I need to know what you want to do, Vash," Bryce said, interrupting her thoughts. "The Barnes Group is giving us twenty days to finalize the deal or they will withdraw their offer."

Vashti stood up to cross the kitchen floor and put her teacup in the kitchen sink. "Okay, I'll think about what you said. Ten million dollars is a lot of money."

"Yes, and just think what you could do with it."

Vashti was thinking and she loved all the possibilities. Although she loved her job, she could stop working and spend the rest of her life traveling to all those places her aunt always wanted to visit but hadn't, because of putting Shelby by the Sea first. Vashti wouldn't make the same mistake.

THE NEXT MORNING, for the first time in two years, Vashti woke up feeling like she was in control of her life and could finally see a light—a bright one at that—at the end of the road. Scott was out of her life, she had a great job, but more importantly, some developer group was interested in her inn.

Her inn.

It seemed odd to think of Shelby by the Sea as hers when it had belonged to her aunt for as long as she could remember. Definitely long before Vashti was born. Her parents' home had been a mile away, and growing up she had spent a lot of her time at Shelby; especially during her teen years when she worked as her aunt's personal assistant. That's when she'd fallen in love with the inn and had thought it was the best place in the world.

Until…

Vashti pushed the "until" from her mind, refusing to go there and hoping Bryce was wrong about her having to return to Catalina Cove to face off with the rezoning board. There had to be another way and she intended to find it. Barely eighteen, she had needed to escape the town that had always been her safe haven because it had become a living hell for her.

An hour later Vashti had showered, dressed and was walking out her door ready to start her day at the Grand Nunes Luxury Hotel in Manhattan. But not before stopping at her favorite café on the corner to grab a blueberry muffin and a cup of coffee. Catalina Cove was considered the blueberry capital in the country, and even she couldn't resist this small indulgence from her hometown. She would be the first to admit that although this blueberry muffin was delicious, it was not as good as the ones Bryce's mother made and sold at their family's restaurant.

With the bag containing her muffin in one hand and her cup of coffee in the other, Vashti caught the elevator up to the hotel's executive floor. She couldn't wait to get to work.

She'd heard that the big man himself, Gideon Nunes, was in town and would be meeting with several top members of the managerial and executive team, which would include her.

It was a half hour before lunch when she received a call to come to Mr. Nunes's office. Ten minutes later she walked out of the CEO's office stunned, in a state of shock. According to Mr. Nunes, his five hotels in the States had been sold, including this one. He'd further stated that the new owner was bringing in his own people, which meant her services were no longer needed.

In other words, she'd been fired.

CHAPTER TWO

A week later

VASHTI GLANCED AROUND the Louis Armstrong New Orleans International Airport. Although she'd never returned to Catalina Cove, she'd flown into this airport many times to attend a hotel conference or convention, or just to get away. Even though Catalina Cove was only an hour's drive away, she'd never been tempted to take the road trip to revisit the parish where she'd been born.

Today, with no job and more time on her hands than she really needed or wanted, in addition to the fact that there was ten million dollars dangling in front of her face, she was returning to Catalina Cove to attend the zoning board meeting and plead her case, although the thought of doing so was a bitter pill to swallow. When she'd left the cove she'd felt she didn't owe the town or its judgmental people anything. Likewise, they didn't owe her a thing. Now fourteen years later she was back and, to her way of thinking, Catalina Cove did owe her something.

*Scandal! The mayor's sister is marrying his nemesis!
Except it's just a rumor, and now the heiress needs
a real husband, fast. Enter her brother's sexy
best friend, security expert Emmett Keaton. It's the
perfect convenient marriage...until they can't keep
their hands to themselves!*

Read on for a sneak peek of
A Christmas Proposition *by Jessica Lemmon,
part of her* Dallas Billionaires Club *series!*

His eyes dipped briefly to her lips, igniting a sizzle in the air that
had no place being there after he'd shared the sad story of his past.
Even so, her answering reaction was to study his firm mouth in
contemplation. The barely there scruff lining his angled jaw. His
dominating presence made her feel fragile yet safe at the same time.

The urge to comfort him—to comfort herself—lingered. This
time she didn't deny it.

With her free hand she reached up and cupped the thick column
of his neck, tugging him down. He resisted, but only barely, stopping
short a brief distance from her mouth to mutter one word.

"Hey..."

She didn't know if he'd meant to follow it with "this is a bad
idea" or "we shouldn't get carried away," but she didn't wait to find
out.

Her lips touched his gently and his mouth answered by puckering
to return the kiss. Her eyes sank closed and his hand flinched against
her palm.

He tasted…amazing. Like spiced cider and a capable, strong, heartbroken man who kept his hurts hidden from the outside world.

Eyes closed, she gripped the back of his neck tighter, angling her head to get more of his mouth. And when he pulled his hand from hers to come to rest on her shoulder, she swore she might melt from lust from that casual touch. His tongue came out to play, tangling with hers in a sensual, forbidden dance.

She used that free hand to fist his undershirt, tugging it up and brushing against the plane of his firm abs, and Emmett's response was to lift the hem of her sweater, where his rough fingertips touched the exposed skin of her torso.

A tight, needy sound escaped her throat, and his lips abruptly stopped moving against hers.

He pulled back, blinking at her with lust-heavy lids. She touched her mouth and looked away, the heady spell broken.

She'd just kissed her brother's best friend—a man who until today she might have jokingly described as her mortal enemy.

Worse, Emmett had kissed her back.

It was okay for this to be pretend—for their wedding to be an arrangement—but there was nothing black-and-white between them any longer. There was real attraction—as volatile as a live wire and as dangerous as a downed electric pole.

Whatever line they'd drawn by agreeing to marry, she'd stepped way, way over it.

He sobered quickly, recovering faster than she did. When he spoke, he echoed the words in her mind.

"That was a mistake."

Don't miss what happens next!
A Christmas Proposition by Jessica Lemmon,
part of her Dallas Billionaires Club series!

Available December 2018 wherever
Harlequin® Desire books and ebooks are sold.

www.Harlequin.com

HDEXP1118

Want to give in to temptation with
steamy tales of irresistible desire?

Check out **Harlequin® Presents®**,
Harlequin® Desire and
Harlequin® Kimani™ Romance books!

New books available every month!

CONNECT WITH US AT:

Facebook.com/groups/HarlequinConnection

 Facebook.com/HarlequinBooks

 Twitter.com/HarlequinBooks

 Instagram.com/HarlequinBooks

 Pinterest.com/HarlequinBooks

ReaderService.com

**ROMANCE WHEN
YOU NEED IT**

PGENRE2018

Love Harlequin romance?

DISCOVER.

Be the first to find out about promotions,
news and exclusive content!

f Facebook.com/HarlequinBooks

🐦 Twitter.com/HarlequinBooks

📷 Instagram.com/HarlequinBooks

📌 Pinterest.com/HarlequinBooks

ReaderService.com

EXPLORE.

Sign up for the Harlequin e-newsletter and
download a free book from any series at
TryHarlequin.com.

CONNECT.

Join our Harlequin community to share
your thoughts and connect with other
romance readers!
Facebook.com/groups/HarlequinConnection

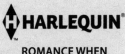

HARLEQUIN®

**ROMANCE WHEN
YOU NEED IT**

HSOCIAL2018

Earn points on your purchase of new Harlequin books from participating retailers.

Turn your points into **FREE BOOKS**
of your choice!

Join for FREE today at
www.HarlequinMyRewards.com.

Harlequin My Rewards is a free program (no fees) without any commitments or obligations.

MYR